*Weekly Reader Children's Book Club presents*

# A LOOK OF EAGLES

WEEKLY READER
CHILDREN'S BOOK CLUB

This is a registered trademark

# A LOOK
## OF EAGLES

BARBARA BERRY

ILLUSTRATED BY W. T. MARS

THE BOBBS-MERRILL COMPANY, INC.

INDIANAPOLIS    NEW YORK

THE BOBBS-MERRILL COMPANY, INC.

PUBLISHERS   INDIANAPOLIS   NEW YORK

*TO  WARREN*

# ONE

FOG DRIFTED in through the open stall door. Sam Johnson yawned, tried to rub the sleep from his gray eyes, and reached under the horse's belly for the saddle girth. He was used to getting up early to work the horse, but cold, dismal mornings like this one were hard to wake up to.

Small for thirteen, Sam had to stand on his toes and hold up the saddle flap with his head to push the billet strap through the girth buckle. The damp leather slipped and the cold made his fingers clumsy, so when he tightened the girth he yanked harder than he intended. Kentucky Colonel, the big bay Thoroughbred, grunted in protest.

"Easy, lad," Gramp said as he came into the stall and took the horse's bridle.

Sam smiled at his grandfather, then ran his hand over Colonel's muscular hip and gave him a friendly slap. "All set," he said. Gramp led Colonel out into the chill mist.

Sam followed them, shivering, as he watched Colonel's low-headed, spiritless plod. Colonel sure wasn't much of a horse, but he was the only horse he and

Gramp had left now. And it was early yet—only April. Maybe Colonel would surprise everybody and come on strong this year. Sam hurried his pace and caught up with Gramp.

"Think we've got any chance at all in today's race?" he asked, shaking his blond hair out of his eyes.

The old man, bundled up to his chin against the cold, showed all six of his remaining teeth in a good-natured grin. "You've always got a *chance,* Sam!" Then he shook his head. "But to tell you the truth, I'd be pretty happy today with third. That's a good field he's up against."

Sam sighed. Well, they said every horse had at least one winning day. Maybe today would be Colonel's.

At the entrance to the track Gramp gave Sam a leg up and squeezed his blue-jeaned calf. "Just take him along easy," he said. "You know Colonel—he can blow it all in the morning if he once gets under motion."

Sam nodded, yawned again, and kicked off. He held his bat ready. "Easy" or not, Colonel would need encouragement. They moved slowly out onto the track. Sam could hear another horse out early, too, somewhere on the other side of the oval. Spring was slow in coming to Ohio this year, and the fog was really bone-chilling. It was still too thick for him to see farther ahead than a post or two.

He rode Colonel's swinging, loose-legged trot once around the track and then hupped him into a lope. The eight-year-old gelding felt so good that he arched his neck playfully. He even shook his head as if he were about to take the bit and run. Sam smiled at the bluff, wishing Colonel really did have that much spirit.

After trotting a full mile, Sam stood forward and

urged Colonel into an easy, collected hand gallop, counting posts to judge his pace. He knew precisely how far Colonel should gallop to get loosened up, and how fast he could run without using up his race. That was what made it all so dull. That, and the fact that it was all so useless. He and Gramp had tried every kind of workout known to racing science, and still Kentucky Colonel was a morning glory. He showed some speed in the mornings, but in the afternoons, when it counted, he just simply didn't have it, or didn't want to use it. Let's face it, Sam thought, he doesn't have much of it in the mornings, either. Well, he was better than an empty stall, as the saying went.

As the big horse galloped through the mists, Sam counted posts mechanically and daydreamed. In his imagination he was riding his favorite dream horse, a fiery, unbeatable stallion. It was the biggest race of the year, and Ted Atkinson was gaining on his right while Willie Shoemaker was trying to sneak through on the rail. They were riding two of the best horses in the country. Sam's stallion, however, was holding his lead easily. They were approaching the stands now, and the enormous crowd was bellowing. . . . Atkinson and Shoemaker were making their last, desperate moves. . . . The stallion sensed it, began to turn on, to pull away. . . . Sam raised his bat and brought it down hard on the stallion's steaming flank, urging him on. . . .

Beneath Sam, in cold reality, Colonel suddenly leaped forward, his neck out, charging for all he was worth. Four posts sped by before Sam could bring him back down to a good workout speed.

Sam clenched the rein furiously. If only somehow he and Gramp could get hold of a *real* horse! One that

10

could take a couple of extra furlongs without getting the heaves or something. One that didn't have to be babied and nursed along to keep it sound. One that could *win*.

Sam finished the workout, then jogged back to the track entrance, where Gramp took the rein. Sliding down, he leaned against Colonel's warm barrel and sighed. Gramp put a gnarled hand on his shoulder. "What were you up on this time?" he asked kindly. "Citation? Man o' War?"

Sam just gave his grandfather a sheepish grin in reply and got busy loosening the girth.

"Now that was a horse," Gramp said. "Big Red— that's what everybody called Man o' War. I saw him run once, when I was about your age. Never forget it. Belmont. Every other entry was scratched after Red beat the world's record in his workout that morning. Nobody expected to beat him anyway, but nobody wanted his own horse to look *that* bad! Well, Mrs. Jeffords, she was a real good sport about it. She sacrificed her colt, Hoodwink, just so it wouldn't be a walkover. Clarence Kummer was up on Red that day. He tried to hold him in—the least he could do for Mrs. Jeffords—but Red wouldn't be held. No, sir. Kummer stood up in his stirrups and hauled on that horse all the way around the track, and he *still* broke two more records and came in a hundred lengths to the good!" Gramp shook his head. "Think of that, Sam. A hundred lengths! And Hoodwink was a fine colt, too."

Sam pulled the saddle off. "So was Temp," he said before he thought. Temper Tantrum had been Gramp's "one good one," a promising two-year-old that was killed in a barn fire.

11

"I know," Gramp said. "It doesn't seem right, sometimes, or fair. But we got to do the best we can with what we got, don't we?"

"Sure," Sam agreed, ashamed of his impatience. He walked beside his grandfather toward the shed row. Colonel, blowing a little from his unscheduled "race," followed along behind. "Someday we'll get another good one," Sam said. "And with you training him and me riding him, how can we lose?"

Gramp nodded. "If Colonel here can just come through for us a couple of times, get us some real money . . ."

He didn't have to finish. They both knew the dream. It was what they lived on.

# TWO

A HEAVY mist also hovered over Winfield Stud in Kentucky hundreds of miles away, wrapping the barns in a soft gray blanket.

Winfield Stud, a famous Thoroughbred nursery, was one of two farms kept by J. S. Winfield III as a hobby. When the Stud's colts and fillies became yearlings, the exceptional ones were sent to Mr. Winfield's farm in New York for training. The others went to the spring yearling sale in nearby Glenview, where they were bought by less wealthy owners hoping for a bargain.

On this dark morning, beyond the soft light of the shaded bulb over a foaling box, the other Winfield mares were still dozing in the quiet of early dawn. But Silver Lining, the mare in the foaling box, was wide awake. A long vigil was coming to an end at last.

So full with foal now that her hide stretched drumlike over her belly, she moved restlessly across the large stall. Her small hooves stirred up a faint rustling in the bedding, a sound that could not have been heard more than a few feet away.

Yet the stud groom, though he was sound asleep in the next stall, awakened at the tiny stirring. Silver

Lining's first foal was on the way. He'd been expecting that sound for the last four nights. He lay there listening. After thirty years with horses, he knew better than to go bounding in. Some mares preferred solitude and would even hold back until they were alone. But others demanded a friendly presence. He waited, holding his breath, until he heard the muted whicker, like a tiny whimper, the sound that meant she wanted company and reassurance. He sighed, pushed back the warm blanket, pulled on his boots and reached for the foaling kit. Company and reassurance she would have, then.

Buttoning up a wool sweater, he let himself into the box stall quietly. As he set the kit on top of the doorpost, Silver Lining hurried over to him, her dark eyes puzzled and forlorn. He stroked her head gently and tried to comfort her. "It's all right, mare. Soon you'll be able to roll all the way over again—think of that."

She seemed eased by his presence, but she was too restless to remain still for long. Heading for the other side of the stall, she snatched fitfully at the hay in the rack. The night was cool and there were no flies, but the mare was sweating heavily, switching her tail and stamping. The groom leaned against the doorway and watched her with concern.

There was something about this foaling business that always got to him, even after thirty years. His pulse quickened as unbidden pictures flashed through his mind: of the occasional foal, brought forth after hours of anxiety and effort, that never drew breath; of the occasional mare that was lost. He chased away those thoughts and reminded himself of all the easy ones, and all the sturdy, alert foals. Each and every one of them was a potential Triple Crown winner—for a while, at least. Take this one, now. Both parents stakes winners . . .

His musings were interrupted as Silver Lining, her coat nearly black with sweat now, lowered herself heavily onto the straw. She stretched out her neck and rested her head on the bedding, only to raise it again immediately, drawing her hind feet up to her belly.

The groom approached her slowly and knelt down by her drenched head. "Just a few more minutes now," he said.

Twelve minutes later the foal had fully emerged. The groom had been tempted, as always, to rush to help it, but he had a great deal of confidence in nature, so he stayed where he was and watched closely. Without any help from anybody the newborn thrust out a soft, waxy hoof and broke through the clear sac that enclosed its body like a cellophane bag. Then it raised its head, straightened its plastered-down ears, sneezed—and breathed.

The groom also breathed, gustily. Now came the close inspection. He walked over to where the foal lay in a heap. The big head waved back and forth vigorously as the foal tried to balance it on the thin stem of a neck. The foal was alive, all right. But was it okay? The groom braced himself and bent down to find out.

It was dark gray—no surprise, coming from two gray parents. Big, too. He pulled the foal a little away from the mare so that she wouldn't step on it if she decided to get up. Then he slipped the rest of the sac off the foal. Most of the cord fell away by itself. The little foal fought briefly against the kind but alien hands. Very good—that showed spirit and alertness. Only when the groom's expert hands had quickly and deftly

15

gone over every inch of the newborn did he allow himself the relief of a wide smile, the smile that had been building up in him since the foal first moved and breathed. He sat back on his heels for just a moment and let his heart fill with gratitude.

But there was still business to attend to. He stood up, fetched down the medicine kit, and opened the jar of iodine paste, briefly touching the three-inch stump of cord into it to prevent infection. The foal winced and he patted it sympathetically. He removed the sterile packing from an already loaded syringe, and with almost the speed of light he gave the foal an antitetanus shot in the hip. This time it flinched wildly, and Silver, who until now had shown no interest in her foal or even any knowledge of its existence, lifted her head and whickered sharply.

"For its own good," the groom said as he glanced up at her. He pushed the foal upright on its still-folded legs, holding it steady as it threatened to flop back on its side. Silver's curiosity grew. She struggled to her feet and turned to face them, her nostrils fluttering and her ears working rapidly. She seemed surprised.

"This is it, all right," the groom chuckled. "Your first son, and a whopper, too." He turned the foal's face toward its mother. "Sudden Storm, say hello to your dam," he told the foal. "She doesn't recognize you yet!"

The mare, more inquisitive now, took a step toward them. The groom rose quickly, releasing the foal. He let it lie where it fell back and led Silver Lining cautiously toward her colt. There was no telling how a mare might react the first time. Silver wasn't even quite certain yet what it was, let alone how she should behave toward it.

As Silver and the groom watched, the gray colt made a tremendous effort and raised himself up onto his folded knees and hocks. He tossed his head overconfidently and lost his balance, toppling over on his side again.

The sudden movement aroused Silver Lining's interest, and the groom let her have her head, keeping his hand close to her halter. First she snuffled the colt all over. Then she began to chew on one of his big legs to encourage him to try to stand up. The colt looked annoyed and jerked away from her. Who

wouldn't? the groom thought. The colt was shivering with cold, after being used to blood heat; he'd been swabbed with iodine and jabbed with a needle; and now his own dam was munching on his leg. Quite a welcome!

Silver persisted, gnawing away on each of his legs and sharp hooves until finally, in irritation and self-defense, the colt tucked them all under him—and lurched to his feet. He weaved and tilted, but he stood for the first time.

The infant racehorse's heavy-lashed, luminous eyes stared at the huge dark shape of the mare he knew instinctively to be the source of food and comfort, and at the much smaller shape of the man, who, just as instinctively, he distrusted. Then, just as he was about to collapse, the smaller shape came forward and supported him. The colt still stood.

Sudden Storm wasn't much to look at. Every bone in his body was clearly outlined. His mane was a succession of tight black curls flopping in alternate directions. His tail was a damp wisp of hair that could have belonged to a squirrel. His tiny muzzle sprouted a beard of curling, faintly goatlike whiskers. He looked, in fact, like a dark, dappled gray baby mule.

Suddenly, propelled by nothing more than momentum and guided by nothing much at all, he charged the width of the stall. The straw and his lack of coordination combined to trip him up. He tilted wildly a few times before cartwheeling over backward and folding up against the wall.

Alarmed, Silver hurried to him. She nudged him once or twice, but he was busy resting, gathering all his forces for his next venture. When the groom tested the mare by moving abruptly toward the colt, she

18

snaked her head at him in stern warning. He knew then that he could leave them alone. Silver Lining had mysteriously joined the ranks of protective mothers, and Sudden Storm was as strong a colt as the groom had ever seen.

He rubbed his tired eyes. Yes, sir—as strong a colt as he'd ever seen. Another Winfield horse was on its way.

# THREE

FOUR weeks later, the eyes of a stable boy warmed as he leaned over Silver Lining's stall and watched Sudden Storm nursing. The colt drank loudly, confidently and roughly. Occasionally Silver Lining winced and grunted and nipped her offspring's rump as a mild reproof, which improved his table manners for a moment. But soon he was tugging too heartily again and the mare became impatient and stepped away from him. The colt's head flew up high; he eyed the boy alertly, and then in a sudden explosion of energy he galloped around the stall. He slipped, went down in a tangle of legs, bounded up again as though nothing had happened, and kicked his mother in the side. She ignored him and went to the boy to get her ears rubbed.

He obliged absently as he gazed down the length of the barn. Two other boys were hanging over a stall door, talking in subdued voices. Half a dozen grooms, their chores done, were squatting, leaning and teetering on their heels in the open doorway enjoying the spring sunshine.

The stud groom came into the barn, squinting as his eyes adjusted to the gloom of the interior. He asked if all the paddocks were clean and, when told that they were, suggested that some of the foals be turned outside for a while.

At the prospect of letting the foals outdoors for the first time, the boys roused to life. At first only one mare and her foal were allowed in the big paddock at once. Later on the animals could mingle, but the foals represented a big investment, and a sharp kick out of jealousy or the joy of release could be disastrous.

The stud groom, who didn't talk much, pointed to Silver Lining's stall first. The boy who had been leaning on the door opened it and took the mare by the halter. He attached the lead strap that always hung by every stall door and led her out into the aisle.

Sudden Storm turned shy and hung back in the stall. But when he saw his dam's rump disappearing as she was led away, he panicked. He pattered and slid on the cement floor of the aisle until he reached the wide doorway and caught sight of her again, still walking calmly away from him toward a maze of blindingly white boards.

Outside, the sunshine struck the colt for the first time, along with a whole new set of sights, sounds and smells. He leaped into the air, galloped along until he reached his mother, and then, overwhelmed with his new freedom, raced past her. Realizing that he was alone, he lost his burst of courage, turned suddenly, galloped back to the mare, and crashed into her hind legs. After that he stuck to her like a shadow, his big eyes and ears and twitching nose all working at top speed.

When they reached the paddock the boy turned Silver Lining loose at the gate. Delighted at the chance for fresh air and exercise, the mare entered the enclosure at once, trotting around it springily, snorting, her head and tail high.

Sudden Storm had never seen his placid dam act like this before, and for a moment he seemed paralyzed. But his senses were all overstimulated and his growing muscles demanded action. He gave a shrill squeal, rushed through the gate, and bucketed around insanely until he collapsed from weariness and excitement. His world was expanding.

Within a short time most of the new foals received their stable names. They had all been registered at birth by the names that would appear in the Stud Book and on racing programs. But these were too "fancy" for the grooms. As the foals acquired definite characteristics and personalities, the men gave them their "real" names.

Sudden Storm, however, became no one's favorite. He remained Sudden Storm, or more often just "Silver's colt," all summer. He was big and handsome. But big, handsome colts were no novelty at Winfield. Sudden Storm attracted no one's particular attention.

When the foals were all turned out into the small pasture with their dams, the gray was the first to venture far from his mother. Later, as the foals grew, they became bolder, forming their own little "herd." A close observer might have noticed that the gray was the boss. More important, he would have noticed that in charging gallops across the pasture the gray colt frequently put on a burst of speed that left the others far behind.

One day in early fall it became clear to everyone that Sudden Storm was a colt to reckon with.

On the first of September most of the foals were six

months old, and it was time for the ordeal of weaning. Sudden Storm had been eating grass, hay and grain for months, but always with his dam and her supply of sweet milk handy. Now all of a sudden the dams were all taken away to a distant pasture, and he was supposed to "get used to it," along with the rest of the weanlings.

The first obstacle Sudden Storm faced was a board fence about four feet high. While the other foals watched him, he reared up and hooked his forelegs over the top board. He was trying to climb over, but he couldn't manage it: before he could get both hind legs off the ground his forelegs would slide off the fence. He stood for a moment, his ears and nostrils twitching.

Then, springing straight up and reaching hard, he got his forehand over the top plank. And a moment later, his hind legs scrambling frantically, he was over —on the other side! Immediately he set off at a high-stepping gallop for the next obstacle, the lane fence.

"Hey! You can't do that!" one of the men yelled.

His shout brought more men running from the barns. They all watched in amazement as Sudden Storm galloped up to the lane fence, slammed to a stop, then popped over it neatly. In a few seconds, whisking his tail, he vanished over the knoll toward the mare pasture.

The men looked at each other in silence. They'd had horses go over fences before, but never a weanling. And certainly never from a complete standstill.

"Just like a cat!" somebody said. "A big gray cat!"

From that day on, the gray colt took his airings in a stallion paddock with a seven-foot fence, and no one at Winfield ever called him Sudden Storm or Silver's colt again. He was The Cat.

The following spring when the new crop of foals

was beginning to arrive, the yearlings were sorted out into two categories, keepers and sale colts. Mr. Winfield came to the Stud to look them over.

When he and the groom got to The Cat's stall Mr. Winfield shook his head. The gray colt, shaggy now, a lighter gray and distinctly dappled, was simply too *big* for a yearling. He had shot up tremendously over the winter, becoming too leggy, too long in the barrel, and just plain gawky. His owner merely glanced at him before walking on to the next colt. "Send that one to Glenview," he said.

The Cat was a sale colt.

# FOUR

THAT spring Gramp and Sam were also in Kentucky, at a small racetrack. And on this particular April day they found themselves in somewhat unusual circumstances. They had some money.

When night came neither of them could sleep. They sat wrapped in horse blankets in an empty stall, their backs propped up against straw bales, and gloated. They had made a thousand dollars that day.

That wasn't all the money they had, either, because Colonel had finally hit his stride last summer. Three times he'd come in second, and three other times he'd actually won. They could hardly believe it. And today, on the strength of those wins, another trainer had paid one thousand dollars for the used-up horse. With what they'd saved from Colonel's winnings, they now had over five thousand dollars.

"I hated to see him go, though," Sam said through a yawn.

"He was a good ol' horse," Gramp agreed. "But you know as well as I do that he didn't have another good race in him."

Gramp shifted around. The straw-and-horse-blanket

bed did little to protect his aching bones from the damp clay floor of the stall. "So what do you say? You want to quit while we're ahead? That'd be the smart thing, you know."

*"Quit?"* Sam exclaimed. "What would we do then?"

Before Gramp could answer, the stall door opened, letting in a blast of cold April air—and Uncle Jim.

Sam had seen his uncle only a few times in recent years, and it took him half a second to recognize him in the light of the battery lantern on the floor. What was *he* doing here, all the way from New York? At this time of night?

"Jim!" Gramp said, sending Sam an odd, almost sheepish glance. "Glad you could get here! Pull up a bale of straw and sit down!"

The man did as he was told. He was blond, of medium height and middle age, and his "city clothes" contrasted oddly with his farmer's wind-reddened face and muscular build. He perched uncomfortably on the straw bale, his hat beside him; he didn't seem to know what to say. Sam, silent and vaguely suspicious, looked from his grandfather to his uncle and back.

"I called Jim last night, Sam, and told him our good news," his grandfather said after a moment.

Uncle Jim smiled at Sam. "I hear you made a killing on that old horse."

"Yeah," Sam said, his gray eyes gazing steadily and accusingly at his grandfather.

Gramp pulled his blanket around his shoulders more snugly. "Yes, well—you see, Sam, we were wondering if maybe . . . " His voice trailed off as he saw Sam's face grow taut.

Sam guessed what was happening. First, Gramp's

unheard-of suggestion that they "quit while they were ahead," and now Uncle Jim's "surprise" visit. It was a plot to get him to go live with Uncle Jim and Aunt Julia!

Hastily Uncle Jim said, "A dairy farm isn't all *that* bad! You're fourteen now—almost fifteen—you really ought to be settled down. Go to the same school all the time and that kind of thing. Your Aunt Julia and I—"

"Gramp," Sam interrupted quietly, "are you quitting on me?"

Gramp picked up a piece of straw and started splitting it with his thumbnail. "I want to be fair to *you,* Sam, that's all. I'm pret' near seventy, and my heart ain't all that good. I could drop over any minute, and then where'd you be?"

Sam was watching Gramp intently, and he was relieved to see that his grandfather didn't mean a word he was saying. Oh, everything he said was true enough, but Sam knew all that wasn't any more important to Gramp than it was to him. He and Gramp understood each other, and how it was with horses and racing and traveling around to the tracks . . .

Gramp looked up just in time to see Sam start to smile, and that did it. He broke out in his six-tooth grin.

"When you drop over," Sam said, "*then* I'll go live with Uncle Jim."

"Now, wait a minute, Dad," Uncle Jim protested. "You agreed on the phone that you should both settle down. That's why I took the first train for Lexington! Before you could change your mind! You can't go on living like this forever—hand to mouth. Why, you win a cheap little race so you can pay your board bill and feed bill and shoeing bill, and then you're wiped out again. It's time both of you grew up and started to live like civilized people."

"I know, Jim," Gramp said. "I know what I said. And I suppose it's right. All these years since Sam's dad got killed—well, we've really had ourselves a time. But I thought maybe now he's older and we're a little ahead of the game for once— I guess not, though. I guess Sam's got horse blood, same as me."

28

Uncle Jim looked at them like a schoolmaster facing two stubborn pupils. "I just can't understand you, Dad. After all the trouble horses have caused for us! And you get me all the way down here, hoping you'd seen reason at last, and then— Well, I suppose *legally* I could—" He saw their faces and stopped. Then he went on in exasperation, "All right, then! *Take* your money and blow it on another horse. That's all that'll make you really happy!" His expression softened a little as he stood up. "I might as well catch that early train back, then. That kid I hired to take care of the cows while I'm gone isn't as smart as he could be. But, Dad—at least you *will* take care of yourself, won't you? Call me right away if you have any problems?"

Gramp nodded, trying not to look *too* pleased with the way things were turning out.

Uncle Jim put on his hat and started to leave, but at the door he turned back. "I've got to ask," he said. "What in the world did you cut that boy's *hair* with?"

"Borrowed some clippers," Gramp mumbled.

"*Horse* clippers?" Uncle Jim laughed.

"Yep."

"I should've known," Uncle Jim said, closing the door behind him.

"Well!" Sam said as soon as they were alone again.

"Tell you the truth, Sam, it wasn't exactly my idea for him to run down here."

"I figured he must've talked you into it."

"He's good at that. Made me feel like a bum, dragging you all over the country like this. And made me feel about a hundred years old, too. But I guess maybe I got a *few* good years ahead of me, before I got to be turned out to pasture."

29

"With all those cows!" Sam laughed and added, "I guess he means well."

"Tell you one thing. Maybe it wouldn't be a bad idea to invest some of that cash in a couple of those folding cots to sleep on! And I was going to ask you— what do you think about buying Stan's old two-horse trailer? He only wants three hundred for it, and it'd save on having to hire rides all the time. We'd have to fix it up some."

"Good idea."

"You do want to keep on, then? Get us another horse?"

Sam leaned forward, his pale hair falling across his eyes. "Are you kidding, Gramp? Quit, just when we finally have a real chance?"

Gramp peered at him across the lantern glow. He'd had too many "chances" that didn't pan out. "Now you got to realize," he said carefully, "that we have to save some, to pay the bills. We can't blow it *all* on a horse."

"How much can we spend?" Sam asked, excited.

"Maybe a couple thousand."

Sam looked disappointed. "What can we get with that? Another Colonel?"

"Yeah, we could pick up another plater. Or we could back a *real* long shot. A yearling. A *cheap* yearling, Sam, but with a chance."

"A yearling." Sam bit his lip, thinking. "It'd be another year before it could race, and it would cost a lot to train it, what with barn bills and track fees." He was quiet for a moment. "Do I look old enough to get a job?" he asked suddenly.

Gramp smiled. "You're kind of undersized."

"All exercise boys are," Sam said, his enthusiasm growing. "At two bucks a gallop, plus walking hots—"

"Wouldn't hurt me to walk a few myself," Gramp added. "Good for the rheumatism."

"A yearling, then?" The boy's eyes were shining.

"A yearling, then."

"How about Glenview?" Sam asked. "That's next week."

"Glenview's a pretty rich sale for the likes of us," Gramp said. "Don't too many two-thousand-dollar yearlings go through there. But I suppose we could just go *look*," he added, his own eyes shining more than a little.

# FIVE

NO SOONER had Sam and Gramp climbed out of their pickup than they ran into an old friend, Pete Barstrom, who waved a sale catalog in their faces.

"Lookit this!" he announced. "Winfield's got thirty-two yearlings consigned this year!"

Sam reached for the catalog, but Gramp put a restraining hand on his arm. Even Winfield's culls—the yearlings they considered inferior and not worth training—were expensive. "Now, then," he cautioned, "Winfield's a long ways out of our reach, Sam. We just come down here to look, remember?"

"They got some beautiful colts in there," Pete said.

Gramp glared at him over Sam's head. "Sure!" he snorted. "And any of that stuff goes for under ten thousand, *I'll* be surprised."

Sam was too excited by the magic name of "Winfield" for Gramp's cautioning to have any real effect. His mind was soaring with visions of glory. "Just think, Gramp! If we had a Winfield colt! Just think!"

"Now *you* just think. First, we ain't got that kind of money. Second, we have to eat." Then he added gently, "Don't fret, Sam. We'll find us a real nice colt someplace for two thousand."

Gramp could see that all those Winfield colts and fillies up for grabs had gone to Sam's head—thirty-two was an unusually large number for them to sell in one year—and now he wished they hadn't come here, even just to look. With all these expensive horses around, how would Sam ever be satisfied with one they could afford? The boy *had* to have his heart in the horse they bought, or it wouldn't be any good.

"Where they got the Winfield stuff?" Sam asked.

Pete pointed to Barn Ten.

"Let's go see, Gramp! It can't hurt to just look, can it?"

Gramp shrugged. By now Sam and Pete had moved off toward Barn Ten anyway. The trouble was, Gramp knew it *could* hurt.

Barn Ten was reserved for the better horses, where each one enjoyed a loose box. Tacked on the front of every box was a typed sheet with the horse's pedigree. It was impossible to get close to the stalls because of all the men who were crowded in front of them, looking at the horses and discussing the pedigrees.

Sam worked his way down the center aisle through the crowds, but Gramp stayed behind, standing in the doorway surveying the entire barn. Seeing one stall with no one at all in front of it, he went to have a look.

First he studied the pedigree, the most important thing about any yearling, and was surprised by what he read. With bloodlines like these, the horse should have had a mob gathered around him. Peeking inside, Gramp saw the biggest, most ungainly rawboned over-legged yearling he'd ever seen. When The Cat looked back at him, Gramp was startled to see the same expression he had seen in only one other horse some fifty years ago, a red colt named Man o' War. It was the bold, imperious look about the eyes that all horsemen search for and few ever find, *the look of eagles*.

Gramp turned away and took a deep breath. He was shaken by the thoughts that had began to run wild through his head. Was it possible that no one else had seen it? Or had he been mistaken? He didn't dare look again and attract attention to the colt. But what if he *was* right, and the colt went for peanuts, as Man o' War had done so long ago? Did he dare hope?

Whistling shakily, he shoved his hands into his pockets as he decided he'd better pretend to look at some of the other stock. He nodded at a man who had walked up to the stall.

"That's a joke, coming from Winfield, ain't it?" The man laughed. "But I guess anybody can come up with a strange one now and then."

Gramp smiled, nodded again in agreement and walked on, whistling.

Gramp said nothing to anyone, certainly not to Sam, whose disappointment showed as the auctioneer worked his way through all the less expensive horses without Gramp even bidding. Finally there was only Winfield stock left.

"You want to leave now," Sam asked, "or stay and watch the rich folks buy the Winfield colts?"

Gramp seemed content to stay where he was. "You in any hurry to go?"

"No. I'd just as soon stay, I guess. Might as well *watch* somebody buy a horse, anyway."

"Fine," Gramp said, ignoring Sam's hint. "I ain't got anything more important to do."

34

Sam sat patiently but without hope as the auctioneer began to run the Winfield yearlings through the ring. While the bidding was spirited right from the first, everyone knew that the best would be saved till last, and the "big boys" from the larger stables were fairly quiet. With a sinking heart Sam noticed that even the cheapest culls were going for six thousand dollars and over. This was a money sale, all right. He understood now why Gramp had warned him.

"This next colt," the auctioneer said then, "is a little rough-looking, but you know if he's a Winfield colt he has good blood behind him, and he'll make somebody a real fine racehorse."

This buildup was lost on his audience, which began to grin and chatter as a weedy-looking gray colt, huge for a yearling, was trotted into the ring with a handler at each side. Sam smiled at Gramp. The idea of this awkward colt on a racetrack was absurd. In just his first circuit of the ring he crossed his long forelegs twice, stumbling over his own feet.

When the rest of the crowd started to snicker, Gramp silently cheered. He couldn't have wished for anything more. Who'd want to bid on a colt everybody was laughing at?

The auctioneer struggled in vain for an opening bid of one thousand dollars while the colt stumbled around, fighting his handlers, and the crowd got louder and more boisterous. Gramp leaned back to have a word with Pete Barstrom, sitting behind them. The auctioneer saw Pete's nod and swiftly knocked down the embarrassing colt for one thousand dollars.

Sam had been too busy laughing along with the others to notice any of this. As the gray was wrestled out of the ring and the crowd settled down, Gramp got up and stretched. "Well, my old carcass has about had it. You ready to go home, Sam?"

Sam got up too and they made their way out between the rows of chairs. Gramp gave Pete Barstrom's shoulder a quick squeeze on the way past.

"I wonder who got stuck with that last colt?" Sam said when they were free of the crowd.

"We did," Gramp said.

Sam stared at him. "*We* did?"

"Yep. Had Pete bid him in for me," Gramp answered calmly. "Thought I'd surprise you. We got us a gen-u-ine Winfield colt, Sam."

Sam's eyes widened as he found his voice. "But he fell all over himself!"

"Sure he did. But I was looking him over before the sale started, and I saw something I liked. You wait."

Sam thought it over silently, his dismay slowly giving way to excitement, while Gramp led the way to the sale office to complete the transaction.

Sam read the pedigree Gramp had handed him as they went on to Barn Ten. His finger traced the ringing, familiar names. He couldn't believe that such a strung-out colt could possibly match this stunning bloodline.

"Sudden Storm," he murmured as they stopped in front of the stall.

The barn was empty now except for a middle-aged Winfield "boy" who had just returned the colt to his stall. "You Mike Johnson?" he asked, wiping the sweat from his face.

Gramp nodded.

"They said you'd be picking him up." He turned to Sam. "His real name's The Cat. Reckon you'll find out why someday. Figure on racin' him, do you?"

"Sure," Sam answered, still clutching the unbeliev-able pedigree.

"He oughta go, all right," the man said. "Too bad he's so homely. Fastest colt in the pasture this year."

Sam and Gramp exchanged pleased looks.

"While he was *in* the pasture, that is," the man added as he left them.

Sam and Gramp pressed up to the barred stall front,

peering inside. The Cat came forward and looked back at them curiously, his ears tilting back and forth, the widened nostrils noisily breathing in their scents.

It was the second time Gramp had seen the colt close up. He had no doubts at all. The colt had it, all right; it was right there in those wide eyes for anybody to see.

And now Sam saw it too. "He's beautiful! The way he *looks* at you—it's beautiful!"

Gramp patted Sam's shoulder, relieved. "You'll do, lad."

Sam turned to him glowing. "The fastest colt at Winfield this year!"

Gramp, more than a little excited himself, said, "There's pretty horses, Sam, and there's fast horses. But you watch this colt. By the time he turns two he'll be the prettiest, *and* fastest, horse you ever saw!"

Sam held the pedigree close. "He's beautiful."

# SIX

TWO months later at a racetrack in Ohio Sam was proudly finishing off The Cat's morning grooming. The horse was standing in front of his stall, cross-tied under the wide overhang. Taking up a stable rubber, Sam gave him a brisk, smooth polishing and whisked away the remaining loose hairs. He was shaking out the rubber as Gramp came around the corner and leaned his arms on the rail that connected the overhang's uprights. Sam held up the old linen cloth, displaying a good-sized hole in the center of it.

Gramp nodded. "I'll get you some more. You needed sponges too, didn't you?"

"I got those when I got paid for working out that filly."

Sam's talents as an exercise boy had been quickly recognized, and no one inquired too closely about his age after they'd seen him ride. The track's racing season was about to open now, and business was booming.

Gramp settled himself comfortably on the rail. "Got any new rides lined up?"

Sam smiled as he considered Gramp's question. "A couple more," he teased, deliberately saying no more, and went on sponging the colt's dark muzzle.

"Well, who? Whose barn you gonna be riding for now?" Gramp asked.

Sam only grinned in reply as he gave the sponge a last *swoosh* down the center of The Cat's face, patted him on the nose and stepped back to admire his work. The Cat, already almost white on his back and sides with a patchwork of dapples over hips and shoulders, had lost his winter coat, and the fine hair held a silvery glitter. His short yearling's mane and tail were black and silver threads. His legs were still charcoal—and still far too big.

"Who?" Gramp prodded impatiently.

"I got into the Whitehall string," Sam said, his face shining. "They'll be up tomorrow."

Even the mediocre string that Whitehall Stable boasted was a large potato. "Whitehall's! Well, now!" Gramp said.

Sam busied himself unsnapping the tie chains while Gramp watched in pleased silence.

The boy was growing fast, Gramp reflected. Had the makings of a jockey for a while there, but not anymore. Like the colt's, Sam's legs seemed to grow an inch or two a day.

Ah, well. There were plenty of jockeys around. It was a mean, tough business to be in anyway. And a trainer, somebody who could really make a horse— now that was a different story. The boy's father would have approved of that even more.

Sam's father had been a real horseman too. Gramp often wondered how he could have sired both sons— Sam's father, the horseman, and Jim, the stolid dairyman.

It takes all kinds, he guessed, sighing as he watched Sam lead the loose-jointed colt into his stall.

He followed Sam and The Cat into the dim interior, snapping the white web stall guard in place behind him. Sam was already on the colt's back, lying there on his stomach and balancing himself across while the colt pulled at the hay in the rack. Gramp took the halter and began to lead The Cat quietly around the stall.

Although they weren't racing anything that year, Gramp and Sam were on the move all summer. As tracks opened and closed for a short racing season, everybody moved, and Sam had to be where the jobs were. They were doing well, though. They had not only kept their original capital, but had even added a little to it. And, although he wasn't earning any money yet, by fall The Cat was under saddle.

First Sam just led him, saddled, on a light snaffle bit and let him play with the jointed metal bar in his mouth. This helped The Cat develop a "soft mouth"—made him more responsive to rein pressure. It also gave him a chance to get used to the feel of the loosely girthed exercise saddle. Sam was impatient and always wanting to go on to the next step in the training, but Gramp kept him back, saying, "He isn't ready yet; don't rush him." Gradually, under Gramp's sharp eye and with his constant cautioning, Sam brought the colt along.

In the summer Sam began exercising The Cat on long-lines and a bitting harness. The harness, a surcingle around the colt's belly with a strap around his tail to hold it in place, had two metal rings on it. Sam ran the long-lines, which were lengths of clothesline with snaps at the ends, from the colt's bit through the rings on the surcingle. This allowed him to guide the colt from the ground. Even before The Cat was strong enough to withstand weight on his back every day, he had already

learned from Sam's groundwork to give easily to the
bit's pressure, rather than resist it, and to steer and stop
handily. Also, from the hours of trotting in wide circles
around Sam on the long-lines, he had begun to develop
good hard muscles and strong lungs.

When Gramp finally gave him the go-ahead, Sam began to ride The Cat two or three times a week for just
a few minutes at a time. He rode him up and down between the barns, walking and trotting, getting the colt
accustomed to the weight and the tight girth, and teach-
ing him to respond to leg pressure as well as rein.

One fall day Sam finished his last exercising job for
the morning. Arms aching from the pull of seven different horses whose trainers hadn't bothered to give them

soft mouths, he trotted excitedly back to the ramshackle shed-row barn at the rear of the grounds that was "home" for the week. Today, at last, they were going to put The Cat on the track for a short, light gallop.

Gramp, almost as excited as Sam, had the colt saddled and waiting. Sam's heart thumped as they led The Cat toward the track. You couldn't tell much about a horse's stride or heart on the long-lines, but when it got out on the track—then you got your first real inkling of what the horse was like. Maybe not the first time out, but soon after. Pretty soon now they'd know. Sam knew Gramp was sharing his nervousness right now, thinking about all their investment in this long-shot colt. For Sam even more was at stake. He loved the big, awkward horse.

On their way to the three-quarter-mile oval the word spread that the Johnsons were going to "unwrap the big colt." The rail began to draw men like a magnet, and soon a small crowd had gathered.

Sam and Gramp took the colt out to the center of the curve and let down the stirrup irons. Then Sam lifted his heel and put it in Gramp's cupped hands. Gramp gave him a leg up and he settled lightly into the saddle, found his stirrups, and gathered up the rein. Unlike most of the coming-two-year-olds, The Cat had been trained to stand quietly for mounting, and the rein hung loose on his neck until Sam picked it up. Some of the men at the rail took this as evidence of a lack of spirit and began to joke about it. "Why don'tcha put him in a Pleasure Horse class, Sam?" one of the exercise boys called out. Sam ignored it all and turned the colt up the track at a walk.

This was important to him, and in spite of all he

could do to loosen up, his muscles remained tense. The Cat felt this. Besides, the colt was excited about the new experience and the thrill of open space. His head high, he stepped along springily, his clean black-tipped ears perked forward with curiosity. He noticed a clump of goldenrod leaning in through the inside rail and arched his neck toward it. As he cross-stepped past to get a good look, he stubbed his toe and stumbled. Again Sam ignored the catcalls from the rail and pulled up The Cat's head to help him recover his balance.

As the colt walked along Sam gave him more and more rein, leaning forward to encourage him. Gently urged on in this way The Cat went into a slow trot. Sam rode it easily, relaxing and going with it, which helped both of them to calm down.

After they had passed a few posts at this soothing pace, Sam got up in his stirrups and urged The Cat into a canter for the first time. The colt broke into the new, rocking gait immediately. He held it, with only one sidewise arc at another goldenrod, until they'd passed the second turn.

The Cat began to get too fresh suddenly, pulling at the bit. Sam remembered Gramp's words: The Cat was to be under complete control all the time. Never was he to go at more than a mild canter, except for that one very short gallop after he was well warmed up. Sam brought him down into a slow trot again. As he passed Gramp at the entrance, Gramp called, "That's fine, Sam!"

Sam let the young stallion canter slowly again past the turn and along the back stretch. The Cat was getting nice and warm now, seeming to enjoy himself without being overexcited about it. He stopped pulling on the

44

bit and began to play with it. His slow, easy canter brought them once more past the onlookers at the rail.

Sam glanced over at Gramp, and the old man nodded his approval. Now he was supposed to canter to the second turn and then let the colt go a little on the home stretch—but keep him well in hand all the way.

His tension returning again at the prospect of the gallop, Sam tightened his grip on the rein. They were approaching the far turn. Almost time now to let him go. Sam leaned farther forward. The Cat felt the rising tension and began to speed up. In the middle of the turn, Sam suddenly whistled shrilly in The Cat's ear.

The Cat responded instantly, his head shooting forward as he lunged. Before Sam could adjust to the abrupt acceleration and begin to pull back, The Cat was charging flat out, his too-big legs reaching, grabbing track, driving powerfully.

Sam knew he shouldn't let The Cat run like that, but he might as well have been pulling back on a freight train. Besides, he'd never ridden a horse at over forty miles an hour before. It was great!

As they pounded past the watching men, Sam could hear Gramp shout, "Will you *look* at that colt go!" Sam grinned, but he knew what Gramp would say later if he didn't get this horse under control pretty soon.

Sam got a good hold on The Cat, braced himself in the irons, and pulled him down to a canter, then a trot, then a jolting, prancing walk. The horse's neck curved sharply and his big hooves were still drumming loudly when Sam rode him back toward Gramp and the rest.

Grinning widely, his heart racing, his hands wet with sweat, Sam brought The Cat to a halt near the entrance. His mood changed instantly when he saw the men huddled around the figure on the ground. "I'll run and call an ambulance," he heard.

Sam slid off The Cat and somebody took the rein from him. As he pushed his way through the knot of men he realized that he didn't see his grandfather. In that moment, he knew something had happened to Gramp.

Reaching the center of the huddle, Sam knelt down beside Gramp. His face was drawn and white, as though he were in terrible pain. Scared and bewildered, Sam took his hand.

Gramp smiled through the pain, and for a moment his eyes shone again. "We really got us one this time, Sam! Didn't I tell you? It's the look of eagles!" His voice was faint and Sam could hardly hear him. He leaned closer, tears welling into his eyes.

"Listen, Sam! Whatever happens, you hang onto that horse, you hear? He's—"

*"Gramp?"*

"You hear me?"

"Sure, Gramp, but—"

Gramp's eyes closed. Sam looked at him for a second, then laid his head down on his grandfather's chest and began to sob. He felt someone lift him up, set him on his feet and lead him away. It was some time before he could accept the fact that Gramp was dead.

# SEVEN

IT WAS a shaken and angry boy who sat beside Uncle Jim on the train the next night on the way to the farm in western New York.

Despite all of Uncle Jim's efforts at conversation, Sam spoke barely half a dozen words the whole time. He alternated between fighting back tears when he thought of Gramp, and clenching his fists until his knuckles hurt when he thought of The Cat. For in spite of Sam's frantic protests, in spite of his promise to Gramp, Uncle Jim had sold The Cat. Now all that Sam had loved was gone. Why? He fretted as the train clacked onward. Why couldn't Uncle Jim have let him keep The Cat? He stared forlornly out at the darkness, bereft and betrayed.

When they reached their station it was well after ten o'clock and they were both exhausted. They got into a Chevy pickup, and since Uncle Jim had given up trying to make conversation, they rode in silence.

"Well, we're home," Uncle Jim said wearily, driving up behind a big white house and parking beside two stake trucks and a car.

The back porch light was flipped on and Aunt Julia

smiled warmly as she held the door open for Sam and led him into a large, bright kitchen.

"So this is Sam," she said, giving his arm a kindly squeeze. "You need some fattening up, but otherwise you look fine. Take your coat off."

Without wasting any more time, she went to the oven and began setting hot covered dishes on the table. Sam was determined to hate this new life, but the aromas that drifted from the table got through to him, and his empty stomach growled in anticipation. He ate silently, but heartily.

Early the next morning, while it was still pitch dark, Sam was roused from his dream-ridden sleep and led out to the huge main barn. In the chill of the morning Uncle Jim showed him around the farm.

The cows—two seemingly endless rows of Guernseys—mooed and grunted as they got up from their beds of sawdust. Sam noticed with surprise that they rose backwards, hindquarters first instead of fore-end first like horses. It gave Sam the odd impression that half the cows were "saying their prayers" as they paused midway in the process, kneeling. Sam didn't know a prize cow from a pig, but his horseman's eye noted that they were all clean, and so was the barn, considering that it had housed fifty cows all night.

Uncle Jim then took him through a door into the milkhouse, which contained a large stainless steel sink and racks with glittering milking machines dangling from them. The big round milk tank stood outside, where an even bigger tank truck would stop soon and draw off the morning's collection. Sam, sullen and still sleepy, took in about half of Uncle Jim's explanations.

When they went back into the barn, Uncle Jim showed Sam how to use an aluminum shovel to fill a big wheeled cart with ground-up grain mix, sticky with molasses. They trundled the cart along in front of the bellowing cows, dumping a pile of feed in front of each one. Sam was fascinated by the unbelievably long pebble-textured pink tongues which set to work scooping it up. He heard little—and understood less—of Uncle Jim's lecture about grain mixes.

After a while Sam became vaguely interested in spite of himself. What he saw and heard convinced him that cows had a pretty soft life. To earn all this food and comfort they had only to produce milk, which didn't cost them any effort at all.

Sam soon found out whose effort *was* required. Back at the milkhouse, Uncle Jim ran a bucket full of warm water and dropped a cloth into it. Then he showed Sam how to pick up and carry one of the milking gadgets. Sam felt like a fool carrying the thing, which looked like some kind of science-fiction octopus with its heavy buckled strap and its one long tube and four short, fat ones. He could guess what the latter were used for.

Uncle Jim, trying hard not to smile at Sam's qualms, showed him how to wash the cow's udder and attach the contraption. After about five minutes of fumbling, Sam managed to get all four of the short, fat tubes to remain on all four teats without falling off. He finished the first one just in time—the cow was beginning to get grouchy —then went on to the next one.

Sam didn't rest until all the cows were milked. When he and his uncle were done at last and had let the cows loose to waddle out to their pasture, it was bright day-

light outside. And Sam was so hungry that when they opened the kitchen door the smell of bacon, eggs and hot cereal was painful.

"How do you like cows?" Aunt Julia asked as he and Uncle Jim washed up at the kitchen sink. "They don't have much personality."

"They're okay," Sam muttered, thinking, well, that wasn't *too* bad.

"He's a real good worker," Uncle Jim said. "We even got some of the other chores done already."

*Some?* Sam sighed.

By midmorning Sam was perched on a towering, racketing tractor, concentrating on Uncle Jim's shouted instructions about two brakes, a clutch and a complicated gearshift lever. By that time he loathed cows, tractors and Uncle Jim with almost equal intensity. For this they had stolen The Cat from him?

Well, he was almost fifteen now, he thought, as he let out the clutch too quickly and was nearly "bucked off." Three more years before he'd be eighteen and could collect the seven thousand dollars plus interest he'd have coming to him from what he and Gramp had saved and The Cat's sale price, and be off on his own. A long wait, but he had no choice. Meanwhile, he would try to find out where The Cat had gone and keep track of him. In a few years, when he was free, maybe he could get his horse back.

School was of no importance to Sam. Until now his education had been a hit-and-miss proposition of enrolling in one school after another while he and Gramp worked the southern racing circuits in the winter. Consequently in New York State with its strict standards, he found himself in the seventh grade with kids one or two years younger than he. But he didn't care. He never talked to anybody unless he had to; he easily did the work assigned to him; and he went straight home on the earliest school bus.

There wasn't a day when he didn't think of Gramp, and miss him, and wonder about The Cat. Still, he couldn't help liking Aunt Julia, whose main purpose in life seemed to be to "fatten him up." Uncle Jim was another story. Uncle Jim was responsible for the loss of The Cat, had forced him to betray his promise to

52

Gramp, and had cheated him out of training and racing the horse that he and Gramp had waited so long to find. No amount of kindness or patience could make up for that.

All winter Sam tried to guess at which of the southern tracks the men he knew might be working. He knew Pete Barstrom had bought The Cat, but where was he? Almost every week he picked a likely track and wrote letters asking for information about The Cat. He knew his chances of getting a reply were slim, as the trainers and owners were constantly moving from one place to another.

One evening Sam was seated at the kitchen table writing to Pete Barstrom again when Uncle Jim came in.

"I thought you had your homework all done," he said, opening the cupboard to get a glass.

When Sam didn't answer, Uncle Jim looked over his shoulder and saw the "Dear Pete." "You still writing those letters, Sam? Why? What difference does it make? Can't you just *forget* it?"

Sam still didn't answer. He leaned farther over his letter, frowning.

The silence was heavy as Uncle Jim walked slowly over to the refrigerator and reached for the milk. "Horses!" he muttered, as much to himself as to Sam. "They killed your father, and then mine. Isn't that enough?"

Sam put his pen down. "No, they didn't," he said, controlling his voice with an effort. "Horses are what kept Gramp going all that time, especially The Cat. You ask anybody, they'll tell you. You should have *seen* him when The Cat—when he—" He lowered his eyes.

Uncle Jim turned around so abruptly that he spilled milk on the floor. "When he got that heart attack! And why? Because he got so excited over that horse! As for your father, you don't know anything about that!"

Sam had not seen Uncle Jim angry since that night at the track. They stared at each other. Then Uncle Jim too lowered his eyes.

"I'm sorry, Sam. Of course you don't know. But, please—no more letters, okay? What's done is done, and I don't want any more horse talk."

Sam never did receive a reply. But he never gave up writing, hoping that one of his letters would connect. He just never mentioned it to Uncle Jim or let himself be caught writing another letter.

# EIGHT

SAM drove a spreader-load of manure out to the rear of the field. He noticed that the trees in the big woodlot that marked the farm's back boundary were sprouting pale new leaves, and he realized it was spring. He shut off the deafening tractor engine and sat for a moment enjoying the silence and the beauty of the budding woodlot.

His mind began to wander. At the tracks now the two-year-olds would be schooling in earnest, galloping and learning about the starting gate. Not The Cat, though. The Cat was big, but he was a late maturer and would need to be brought along slowly. No racing until autumn at the earliest.

Sam caught himself up. That was what he and Gramp would have done with The Cat. But there was no telling who might have him now. His owner might be pushing him too fast, endangering his unknit, juvenile bones and joints with hard workouts . . .

Sam's hands tightened on the steering wheel. What was he doing here, fooling around with stinking, brainless Guernseys? He ought to be training The Cat! Making sure he was watered off slowly enough, that the

track wasn't too hard, that his leg bandages weren't too tight, that he got exactly the right amount of grain mix at exactly the right times!

Sam leaped down from the hot, smelly tractor and walked briskly into the shade of the woods, breathing in the clean, loam-scented air. Feeling suddenly, achingly alone, he sat down on a fallen tree trunk and let the tears come.

After a while he got up and began to wander aimlessly in the spring woods. When he came upon another open field on the opposite side, he thought he'd lost his mind. Right in front of him, not more than fifty yards distant, was a white-railed quarter-mile track.

Sam approached it gingerly. It was too small for a racetrack. It must be a riding ring of some kind, he thought. Looking closely, he found that it *was* a riding ring, well maintained and well used, too. It had recently been disked up and smoothed over. Sam leaned over the low rail and stuck one hand into the surface of the track. The "cushion" was beautiful—lots of sawdust worked into it, and soft to a depth of several inches.

He gazed incredulously across the grassy center of the narrow oval. What an ideal setup this would have been if he had been allowed to bring The Cat with him! There *had* to be horses around here someplace. And Uncle Jim had never said a word, not one word!

Sam walked on until he came to a large unpainted barn beside a dirt road that he hadn't known existed. A tall, slender man waved as he came toward Sam leading a short-legged fat mare through a paddock.

Still only half-believing, Sam waved back and went to meet him.

"Where'd *you* come from, all of a sudden?" the man asked in a friendly way.

Sam pointed backward with a thumb. "Over there. The other side of the woods." He reached out slowly, murmured "Whoa," and stroked the fat mare's neck.

The man smiled. "That'd be Jim Johnson's place, and that makes you Sam. I should've known, anyway, as soon as you touched the mare's neck."

Sam looked at him inquiringly.

"Most people try to pet a horse's nose or face, unless they know horses. And I heard that Jim's nephew had something to do with racing."

Sam grinned. "You sound like you've had some experience with people who don't know horses."

"I get all kinds here, all right. By the way—" He held out a long, slim hand. "—the name's John Craig. And this elegant establishment you see before you is called Craigmoor, God love us. People expect a name like that. 'Craig's Place' would suit me, but it wouldn't impress the public so much."

The man's eyes smiled even when his mouth was still. It was easy to see that he was happy here at Craigmoor. Sam liked him. Also, he hadn't talked to another "horse person" all winter.

"What kind of a setup have you got here?" he asked. "That ring isn't big enough for race training, really, and this mare sure isn't a racehorse."

John laid a hand on the mare's thick mane. "No, old Bess here is hardly a racehorse. But she's the best little school horse for beginners in the world. I give riding lessons to kids who can't afford to go across the lake to Hilltop Farms. It's twenty bucks an hour over there, so at five I'm a real bargain!" He laughed and shrugged his shoulders. "Actually, I give riding lessons because I like to. For a *living*—well, I board a few, and train a few, and one way or another I scrape up the feed bill almost on time every month. It gives me an excuse to stay with horses. I don't think I could live in town—go to work in a factory or something. You know?"

Sam nodded. He felt tears forming in his eyes again and hurried to speak before he disgraced himself. "What're you going to do with Bess?"

John pulled the little mare's topknot straighter through the red-and-white-dotted browband of her bridle. "Just jog her around the ring a few times. I only have three students now. They don't really start coming in till summer vacation, but then I always have more than I can handle. And as you can see, Bess has had her nose in the old feed tub too much. I shouldn't let her get so fat, but she carries on so at feeding time I always give her some grain just to stop her bellering."

He tightened the girth on the cutback show saddle and came around to look at Sam. "I always feel ridiculous on her, though. Her at under fifteen hands and me at six-feet-two! How'd you like to give me a hand today and take her around the ring while I go help the farrier?"

Sam could hear the ring of steel on steel from somewhere near the front of the big barn. He hesitated for a minute, but his great desire to ride again easily overcame his twinge of conscience. After all, Uncle Jim hadn't actually forbidden him to ride. All he'd said was that he didn't want to hear any more "horse talk." And with any luck, Uncle Jim would never have to know. "Sure," he said. "If you want me to."

"Great! Just trot her around until she starts to puff and wheeze. That won't take very long. If I'm not back by the time you're through, I'll be up front." He left, heading for the barn.

Sam stood looking at the bay mare, still trying to believe what was happening to him. All this time there'd been horses practically in his backyard! Before the dull anger at Uncle Jim could build up and spoil this chance for pleasure, Sam mounted the mare and turned her into the ring entrance.

The show saddle took some getting used to, but Sam could see why Bess was such a good school horse. She handled well and had an even, floating trot. She *was* out of condition, though, and she was soon blowing and sweating. Sam slid down and hugged her around the neck. She wasn't The Cat, or even Kentucky Colonel, but she was a real live horse. The coming three years now seemed more bearable. But he'd better get her back and taken care of before Uncle Jim began to miss him.

Leading her through the paddock and up to the rear of the barn, Sam saw a dingy white cooler hanging on the wall just inside. He draped it over the little mare, where it hung almost to the ground, and began to lead her around in the sunshine.

While he walked, he gave the place a good looking over. Everything seemed well used but clean and neatly kept. The barn was old but large and well built; the box stalls inside, while dented, chewed and battered, seemed to be in good repair. The stall fronts that lined the wide center aisle on both sides were hung thickly with tack and training gear. A real working barn, Sam thought.

Through the open barn doors he could see the farrier's pickup truck parked out front and the little forge set up by the front door. John was holding a big gelding's halter while the farrier worked quickly on a hind hoof, packing it with oakum. The glossy horse tried to pull away once, and John reassured it gently with, "You're okay, Commander."

Sam halted the mare and stood watching for a minute. The gelding wore a tail set over its blanket, so Sam figured it must be a Saddlebred in training. All he knew about Saddlebreds was that they were expensive show horses, and that it was a long, complicated process, requiring an expert trainer, to get one ready to show. His curiosity increased, along with his admiration for John Craig.

Sam finished cooling out the mare, battling with his conscience again. But it was an unequal struggle. The

60

urge to be with horses again, given this unexpected opportunity, was just too strong. He knew he'd be spending a lot of time here at Craigmoor from now on. It wouldn't be easy, the way Uncle Jim felt about horses, but he'd have to find a way somehow.

Until midsummer Sam managed to go through the woods to Craigmoor two or three times a week. In fact, using one excuse or another to be out of Uncle Jim's sight for a while, he found it ridiculously easy. Then one day he discovered *why* it had been so easy. He arrived at the horse barn's back door just as Uncle Jim's truck pulled up at the front door!

John was coming out of the tackroom, halfway along the aisle, and he shot Sam a brief "what now?" look before he went to greet Uncle Jim.

"Hi there, John," Uncle Jim said. He *looked* friendly enough, and since Sam knew his uncle had seen him already anyway, he came along to where the two men were standing in the wide doorway.

Neither Uncle Jim nor Sam said anything, and they both looked uneasy, so John finally said, "The coffee's on. Come on in the tackroom, Jim, and maybe we can get this whole thing worked out."

Sam sweated through the endless business with the coffee, the sugar and powdered cream, until all three were seated at last. He wound up sharing the lumpy old couch with Uncle Jim, a saddle upside down between them, while John eased back in his beat-up armchair. Sam's heart almost stopped at John's opening remark.

"I guess you know Sam's been coming over here regularly, don't you, Jim?"

Uncle Jim nodded, and to Sam's surprise and relief, his eyes were crinkling at the corners. "It isn't all that easy to sneak off when you've got to cross a ten-acre open field first."

John laughed. He was relieved too. Sam's "sneaking off" had been bothering him, and he knew it bothered Sam as well. It was good to get things out into the open. "You don't mind, then?" he asked Uncle Jim.

Sam held his breath while Uncle Jim answered slowly and thoughtfully, "Well, yes. I have to admit that I do mind. I'd really just as soon he stayed away from horses for a while, John." He sighed. "As long as possible, anyway. I know they're like a magnet to him."

John stirred his coffee while he considered this. "Of course it's up to you," he said at last. "I'll have to go along with whatever you say. But have you noticed any change in Sam since he started coming over here?"

Uncle Jim smiled thinly. "You got me there. The kid *has* quit moping around so much; there's no doubt about that. And I was getting real worried about him, there for a while."

John pressed his advantage. "He's a natural-born horseman, that's for sure. I'm training a five-year-old stallion that I don't dare turn my back on for a minute, but Sam's got him eating out of his hand."

"I can believe that," Uncle Jim admitted. "His father and his grandfather were the same way."

"So why do you want to keep him away from here, then? He's a big help to me, and I sure enjoy having him around. Doesn't he get his work done on the farm?"

Uncle Jim's smile was wider this time. "Oh, yes— he's a good worker. To tell you the truth, John, I think I really came over so you could talk me into it." The smile faded. "I guess what hurt me most was his sneaking off like that. You could have told me, Sam, and we could've talked about it, at least."

Sam looked down. He refused to show any emotion, either shame at his deception or pleasure at this newly won permission.

Uncle Jim waited a minute for some response, then shook his head and rose, forcing another smile. "Well, just see that you don't let him get you mixed up with horse racing, John!" he joked. "And we'll see how it works out."

After he left, John sat looking at Sam for some time, hoping he'd relent and admit that his uncle wasn't so unfair after all. But he wasn't too surprised when Sam refused to do so. John knew how much The Cat—and his loss—meant to Sam.

"Aren't you ever going to forgive him?" he asked finally.

Sam got up and picked up the saddle. "Oh, sure," he said casually. But the gray eyes held no forgiveness.

# NINE

SPRING had also arrived at a fairgrounds in western Pennsylvania where two men hunkered around the gray colt's forelegs. Neither of them noticed the sweet-smelling air this morning, though the air they were inhaling reeked of liniment.

The Cat's third owner since Sam had last seen him reached out and felt the heat in the left foreleg again. He shook his head. "I'll tell you," he said to the veterinarian, "I just don't know *what* to do with him now."

The vet stood up and sucked in his lower lip, rubbing his chin. "The only way you *might* have him ready to work out again in a few weeks is to fire him, but you know how I feel about that. To me, the only thing to do with a bowed tendon like this is give it a long rest. I think the firing needle ought to be outlawed."

Cutting short the other man's protests, he added, "I know what your problems are. You have to get a horse on the track. So go ahead and fire him, then. You will, anyway."

"That's your advice," the man said.

The vet frowned at him. "My *advice*," he corrected, "is to lay him up on a reduced ration, for a couple of months at least. This won't be his first firing, you know. Look at all the marks on him! He may very well be past ever being sound again."

They regarded the big colt with a feeling of frustration. The Cat had got over his ugly-duckling stage now. He was once again the lithe, beautiful animal he'd been before he started sprouting so fast. But he'd been overworked, and his strained, abused left foreleg was misshapen and swollen.

"I'll fire him this afternoon," the man decided, "and then put him up for three weeks. That's the best I can do."

"He won't be a bit better in three weeks," the vet said angrily. "He'll look better and run better, but as soon as he puts any strain on that leg you'll be blistering and firing again. You'll ruin him."

"It's the best I can do," the man repeated stubbornly. "It's all well and good to be a bleeding heart, but when a horse is eating its head off and the bills are piling up, only a fool or a rich man can let it stand around 'resting.' Business is business."

The vet turned out to be right. The too-early hard galloping, the too-strenuous workouts took their toll by mid-summer, and The Cat was finished. His forelegs were ruined, at least for racing. His owner was heartsick, but his horses had to pay their way or they didn't eat—it was as simple as that.

Besides bowed tendons, The Cat had given his owners other worries in abundance. At first he worked well, apparently eager to run and give all he had. When Sam left, The Cat got used to having different boys up on him after a while. There were even one or two that he seemed partial to.

But one owner after another pushed him too fast, and his overstrained legs started hurting him. Mostly it was his left foreleg, and sometimes it was so painful that he could hardly step on it, let alone run.

The leg had been blistered—"hot" ointment had been applied to irritate the area and increase the circulation of blood, with its healing white cells. But no sooner would The Cat begin to feel better after the blistering than the hard workouts would be resumed, and in a day or two his fast-growing joints and tendons would give way again. Then the firings. The sharp-pointed instrument had jabbed his sore tendons so many times that now The Cat panicked at the smell of the hot electric needle.

The Cat began to resist going out to the track in the mornings. The workouts were too closely associated with pain—the pain of the jarring contact of the hard track on his sore legs, and the subsequent pain of the blisterings and firings.

Then there was the added indignity of the starting gate. His legs hurting, he'd be ridden into one of the narrow stalls. When he had just begun to get used to the confinement, the gate in front of him would burst open with a terrifying clang and he would be given a stinging jolt with an electric prod, to teach him to get out of there fast.

He got out of there fast, yes. But he didn't understand that the gate was mechanical or who was prodding him. So he fought his rider, whom he blamed for all his miseries. Before long he came out of the gate bucking every time, leaving his exercise boy behind him, either sprawled on the ground or hanging over some part of the starting gate.

After several months of this treatment, The Cat acquired "bad legs," an aversion to starting gates that amounted to hysteria, and a fast-growing reputation as a bad actor. Understandably enough, few boys were willing to ride him.

One night, faced with a bill for over fifty dollars for repairs to the starting gate, his latest owner sat down to think it over. It didn't take him long to come to a decision. The colt was as well bred as any Thoroughbred going. He was a striking horse to look at, too, with his silver and black-dapple coat set off by charcoal legs, and his fine, well-balanced conformation. Trotted into a sale ring after a few weeks of rest and heavy graining, he'd catch anybody's eye. He'd just have to send the colt someplace where its reputation hadn't spread yet and put it on the block. The Cat would have to go.

He got a good price for The Cat, from a racing enthusiast from Detroit with more money than horse sense. The two-year-old gray soon changed hands again, though not before another firing, and not before he had become totally unmanageable on the track and had badly crippled an exercise boy. In midwinter, the next time The Cat was sold, the price was considerably lower.

He was purchased as a jumper prospect, and his new owner was a good horseman who often took horses "straight off the track" and turned them into valuable riding horses. For months he worked with The Cat, gaining his confidence, building up his legs and muscles, and finally training him to jump a little.

The Cat took to jumping with enthusiasm. His trainer

was experienced enough not to rush the colt, who was still only two years old. By the time he'd turned three and they were beginning to use the outdoor ring, The Cat was still working only lightly, jumping low obstacles with ease and perfecting his balance, coordination and timing. Most important, he was once again learning to trust a man. Then, with other young horses to start, his owner, deciding that The Cat was ready to sell as a riding horse, took him to an auction. There Jack Barrows, attracted by The Cat's size—almost seventeen hands now—and his heavy muscling, bought him.

Jack Barrows had made his reputation in Puissance classes—"power jumping"—where the obstacles were high and demanded speed, strength and courage. Barrows was also known for getting trophies with a horse, fast, no matter how rough they were. He was *not* noted for his patience.

He was aware that The Cat had once had a reputation as a "behavior problem." But he knew how to deal with behavior problems. He prepared for his first workout with the stallion by having him bitted in a long-shanked curb with a tight chain, and he picked out his heaviest riding crop. The first thing Barrows did was try to provoke a fight with The Cat, feeling that the sooner the horse realized who was giving the orders, the better. He jerked on the harsh bit, spurred the horse's sides, and gave him a few smart raps with the crop.

After the kind treatment he had been receiving lately, The Cat reacted to this sudden abuse by standing motionless, except for the faint quivering of his muscles. In his eyes the look of eagles burned brightly.

Barrows noticed nothing and was very pleased with

himself. He manhandled The Cat through a fifteen-minute warmup, then put him on a track that led around to a high jump. The Cat broke into a gallop, arching his neck to ease the action of the curb.

Barrows saw that the horse was going to rush the jump, but he had no doubt that he could clear it. Instead of trying to pull the stallion down to a reasonable speed, he gave him the whip. Two stable boys standing by the rail watched open-mouthed as The Cat hit the takeoff point at a full gallop and Barrows yelled in his ear. The gray horse soared, clearing the jump easily even though it was much higher than he was used to. But he landed badly, with a hard jolt. Barrows hauled him around and started him on another turn of the ring at a good gallop.

Barrows was elated. Visions of huge trophies flashed through his mind. This was a "power jumper" if he'd ever seen one! Now to put him over it a few more times —fast, before he lost his steam—get him used to charging, then raise the jump higher.

The Cat approached the jump at a terrific speed; again he flew over it with plenty to spare. But the two boys at the rail could see what Barrows could not—the stallion's eyes were getting wild and white-ringed. Every time Barrows yelled, or jerked the bit, or jabbed with his spurs, the horse's eyes grew wilder. By the fourth approach, still at a gallop, the gray's eyes were nearly crazed with fright and anger.

This time he charged at the jump so hard that even Barrows began to have second thoughts. The horse smashed straight through the two rails. They were flung aside and struck the ring fence several yards away.

His knees had been badly knocked, but The Cat continued to charge around the ring, swinging his head from side to side, completely out of control.

Barrows was scared. He'd never before been on a horse he couldn't control. Finally The Cat slowed down enough from his frenzied racing for Barrows to slide off and drag him to a halt. The horse stood panting, the sweat running down his legs.

Embarrassed by his scare and his humiliating departure from the horse's back, Barrows decided that now, while The Cat was tired and winded, was a good time to settle this thing—and save his own face a little. He called sharply to the two boys.

"Fasten those rails down! I want 'em good and solid this time. If he hits it again he'll know he hit something!"

The boys hesitated, but a snarl from Barrows sent them through the fence, where they locked the two heavy rails in place. With wide wings on the standards, the jump was now virtually immovable.

Barrows remounted. With crop and spurs he put the tiring horse into a canter. Circling the ring on weary legs, The Cat approached the obstacle once more. He was an immensely strong horse; he still had plenty of power left to clear this jump, and he began to charge.

But this time he took off several feet too close and dived straight at the top rail, which held for an instant and then snapped loudly, splintering. Horse and rider went down amid the wreckage of the jump.

When the dust began to clear, The Cat was sitting up on his haunches, and Barrows's leg was caught beneath him. The Cat shifted his foreleg, got his hocks under him, and lurched to his feet. The boys climbing through the fence watched in horror as one steel-shod hoof

71

kicked out savagely and caught Jack Barrows on the side of the head, killing him instantly. The boys froze. They'd seen jumping accidents before. What shocked them was the fact that this was no accident. The gray horse was a killer.

# TEN

THE early autumn sun was sliding toward the hilltops. Sam was working Bess, slimmer now, over some jumps he'd set up on the ring's track. Sam didn't share John's enthusiasm for riding show horses. He didn't like the double bridle with its two sets of reins, and he couldn't get used to the Saddlebred's high head set and having to sit back on the cantle of the saddle. He was forever forgetting and leaning forward, smacking his nose on the horse's almost vertical neck and picking its mane out of his mouth. John could keep his Saddle Horses!

He had discovered that Bess could jump one day when just to keep from being bored he'd put a stick across two bushel baskets and tried it. Now he had a variety of jumps for Bess to work out on, made out of oil drums, sawhorses, planks, and even a wheelbarrow —all more or less portable, since John needed the track for the Saddle Horses too.

Sam loved jumping, even on little Bess, whose limit was about four feet high. He loved the exciting approach, and the brief feeling of flight as the mare soared over the obstacle. He didn't even really mind when Bess decided suddenly not to jump and his "flight" was solo.

Sam was feeling particularly good this evening, almost contented. For the past year and a half he'd been working like a dog. School, farm work, and the minute he was free, chores and "horse work" at Craigmoor, not to mention nagging John, who Sam thought was too easygoing. The big old barn sparkled with two new coats of white paint, and the fences, which stood revealed when Sam cut the weeds away, had also been painted.

John had changed, too, becoming more ambitious, more aware of his own worth. Sam had talked him into raising his training fees to more than just come out even, and into raising his lesson fees to ten dollars an hour.

John was working Commander now on the long-lines, in the center of the ring, where Sam had just cut the grass yesterday. Sam decided Bess had had enough and he sat relaxed on her, his feet dangling free of the irons, as he rode her around slowly to cool her off.

John startled him. "Hey! You almost walked that horse right into the fence!" He laughed.

Sam pulled her up. "Thinking," he said. He slid down and they led the two horses back to the barn. "How's Commander doing?"

"Commander's Fanciful Delight," John replied wryly, using the horse's registered name, "is doing just fine, thank you." He patted the elegant gelding on the neck and unhooked the checkrein from the bitting harness. "But he's got the hock action of an arthritic. He'll never send any judges into ecstasies."

Sam, almost as tall as John now and deeply sunbrowned, grinned at his friend. "Why don't you quit wasting your time on these mechanical monsters and get some horses?"

"By that I suppose you mean jumpers? You know, you could be right at that! Sometimes I get awfully tired of trying to keep shoes on these long-toed wonders!"

Sam laughed, well aware that John would never give up his beloved Saddle Horses.

They led the horses into the barn and cross-tied Commander in the wide rubber-matted aisle. While Sam unsaddled Bess and put her away, John removed the gelding's harness, took off the bridle, rinsed the bits, and hung it up. Sam brought over a pail of warm water and they washed Commander, then dried him.

"You know something?" John said when they were brushing the horse off. "You've done miracles with Bess.

I never saw anybody ride over jumps any better than you do. You *deserve* a good jumper, and I really think I'd like to get one."

Sam slid Commander's blanket over him and reached under for a strap.

"I mean it," John insisted when Sam didn't answer. "You should see some of the shows, too. When was the last time you were 'off the farm,' anyway?"

"I haven't been, not since I came here."

"That's what I thought." John buckled on Commander's tail set and adjusted the crupper carefully, making sure the padding was in place. As he looped up the long, thick tail and began to wrap it he said, "Tell you what, I'm taking old leadfoot here to the Youngstown, Ohio, show next week. Why don't you come along? We'll get him through that show, then maybe hit the one in Meadville on the way back. Just have us a good look around. I can get somebody to stay with the rest of the horses, and we'd be back before school starts."

He paused while he put Commander's neck-wrap on. "Frank Peterson says he's ready to buy another gaited horse, so I'll be keeping my ears open along that line, too. Might run across something for him," he added smugly, watching Sam's face. Peterson's horses appeared regularly in the local newspaper, for winning trophies for Hilltop Farm across the lake.

Sam's surprise was plain. "Okay. What've you been up to?"

John laughed. "When I heard Frank was building a new house on this side of the lake I thought, why *shouldn't* I train his horses? I've never had any really big winners, but—"

"But you've never had any top stock to work with,"

Sam interrupted. "That's what I keep *telling* you."

"I know. Well, your nagging worked. I called him up and he stopped in this morning to look us over. And as soon as I—or we—get back from our trip, he's sending them all over here! Four stake horses! Do you realize that's four more than we've ever had here?"

Sam was impressed. "*All* stake horses? That means you'll be going to more shows, doesn't it?"

"You can run things here when I'm gone. Most of the big shows are when school's out. Or we'll get somebody else to stay, if you want to go along."

Sam waited while John put Commander in his stall. The barn was beginning to vibrate with whinnies and irate thumpings announcing the horses' awareness of feeding time.

He was still deep in thought as he stood measuring out grain in the feed room. "You keep saying 'we' and 'us,' " he told John, "like I'll always be around here after next year."

John looked puzzled.

"I won't be able to stay here, you know," Sam said.

There was silence while the two friends, one sixteen and the other forty-two, looked at each other in the growing darkness of the feed room. John reached up and flipped on the light, then picked up a tiger kitten that was rummaging around on the shelf and began to stroke it.

"Why not?" he asked.

Sam scooped out another huge mound of grain mix. "I have to try to find The Cat, you know that."

John sighed and set the kitten on the floor. "I thought you'd given up that idea, Sam."

Since that last day at the racetrack Sam had grown

up a lot and had lost much of his bitterness. But he still loved The Cat, and the fact that he couldn't live up to his promise to Gramp still gnawed at him.

"No," he said finally. "I haven't given it up."

John glanced at the stack of racing sheets in the dusty corner. "You never found his name in any of those, did you?"

"No."

"Well, then. He isn't even racing, probably. He's probably some kid's pet by now. You'll never find him after all this time."

"I've got to try," Sam said grimly.

John let it go. "Well, what about this trip? You want to go or not?"

"Sure, if Uncle Jim'll let me," Sam said, glad for the distraction.

"He will." As John took the pan of grain Sam was holding, the wall on the other side of the feed room was kicked resoundingly. "Maybe we'll even find you a good jumper, somewhere along the way."

Sam laughed awkwardly. "Bribery will get you no-where."

"We'll see," John said. "I'll talk to Jim about the trip if you want me to."

That evening Sam sat at the kitchen table waiting for John to arrive as he'd promised. Uncle Jim poured coffee from the enamel pot on the stove and sat down across from him, while Aunt Julia finished drying the dinner dishes. Sam was a little nervous. He'd told his aunt and uncle only that John was coming over tonight, not saying anything about the show trip. He hoped they'd let him go, but since he'd hardly mentioned Craigmoor or horses to Uncle Jim since that day in the

78

tackroom, he couldn't be sure what Uncle Jim's reaction would be. He'd rather let John ask him about it.

Uncle Jim seemed uneasy too, for some reason, and they'd sat there awhile trying to avoid each other's eyes. Sam was about to go to wait in his room when there was a knock at the kitchen door and Aunt Julia let John in.

"Sorry I'm a little late," he said as he sat down at the table and Aunt Julia set out cups and saucers. "Had one of those visitors at the barn who just won't leave. I thought I'd never get away."

John's breezy personality soon eased the strain that had been building up in the kitchen while they'd waited for him. Sam relaxed a little and let the others talk. But after the usual exchange of information about crops and livestock, the conversation petered out.

Uncle Jim reached behind him for the coffeepot. "Did you have something particular in mind, John?" he asked, filling everyone's cup.

"I'd like to take Sam along with me on a show trip next week," John said. "We'd only be gone about ten days. Sam's worked hard and I think he ought to take a break. Not that I won't keep him busy helping me, but I'm only taking the one horse, Commander, so it's to be more or less a vacation."

Aunt Julia picked up her cup. "That's my favorite TV show coming on now, if you'll excuse me," she said, adding as she went into the living room, "*I* think it's just what Sam needs."

"Well, there's more," John said, glancing at Sam. "I don't know how you're going to feel about all this, Jim, but I'll tell you what I'd like to do. After Sam's through school and has his trust money, if he still doesn't want to go to college I'd like to take him in as a full partner in Craigmoor." He saw Jim's raised eyebrows and rushed on, while Sam nearly popped out of his chair. He hadn't heard anything about *these* plans before.

"We're starting to get somewhere now, and it's been mostly Sam's doing. But that's all a couple of years off yet. What I'd like to do right now is get him over there on more of a full-time basis, allowing for school, of course." He smiled at Sam's astonishment. "I wouldn't want an illiterate partner."

For a moment they all just sat around the table in silence, listening to the theme song of Aunt Julia's TV program and staring down at their cups.

"I guess it's time I made a confession," Uncle Jim said suddenly. Sam and John both looked up.

Uncle Jim's weatherbeaten face took on a melancholy look as he gazed down at the steaming coffee.

"I failed once, a long time ago, and I've been making the boy pay for it." He turned to Sam. "That day your father was killed . . . I was helping him load a colt into the starting gate while he rode it. But I've never been any good with horses, not like your dad was. Always half scared of 'em. And then when that colt played up, knocked your dad off underneath him—it all happened so fast! I *tried* to get him out of there, but I've always wondered. *Maybe* if I hadn't been so scared, I could've jumped in there quicker, you see, instead of having to get my nerve up first. Maybe I could've saved him. Maybe not, too, but you don't ever forgive yourself for hesitating like that. And I guess I've been scared *you'd* get hurt, ever since."

He took a deep swallow of coffee. "I still don't want you to get mixed up with racing, Sam. Those crazy, nerved-up horses. And you've got to be a millionaire to get anywhere in that business—money makes the mare go, all right. But if you want to take John up on what sounds like a real fine offer—well, I certainly wouldn't have any objections."

No one spoke. Sam was trying to understand all he'd just heard and reconcile it with his plans to look for The Cat. John sat drawing circles on the plastic tablecloth with a spoon handle. Uncle Jim was staring down at the table, lost in thought.

There was a burst of laughter and applause from the TV set, and Aunt Julia appeared in the doorway. "Is Sam going?" she asked.

They looked at her blankly. John's plans for the future, and Uncle Jim's story, had driven away all thoughts of the show trip.

"Because if he is," she went on, "I'll have to see about some clothes for him. He won't want to take his new school things, and he's outgrown everything else."

Uncle Jim leaned back, looking greatly relieved. "Sure he's going! He's getting two weeks' vacation with pay, and about time after two years of hard labor!" He stood up and said to Aunt Julia, "Guess I'll hire one of those kids in the agriculture course who're always hanging around begging for a job. Sam's going to be busy over at the stable from now on." He smiled at John. "None too soon, either. I swear if I didn't keep my eye on Sam he'd be trotting my Guernseys around in circles. A dairy farmer he isn't."

Sam's thoughts were jumbled. He felt happy, grateful, and confused. For a moment he couldn't think of anything to say.

"I don't need the two weeks' pay, Uncle Jim," he

said finally. "I've got over a hundred saved up." Then to John, who was reaching for his jacket, "I can pay my own way—the motel bills and stuff."

John laughed. "*Motel* bills? That comes later, when Frank Peterson's paying the expenses! This time we'll be sleeping in a stall on the hay—itchy, but cheap. And Commander won't mind, as long as you don't snore a lot."

"Just so he doesn't roll over in his sleep," Sam said.

# ELEVEN

THE sun shone on the Youngstown, Ohio, horse show. Sam stood at the in-gate of the main ring watching John riding Commander in his first class, for Three-Gaited Saddle Horses. But his attention kept straying to the jump course a few yards away. Quite a crowd had gathered around the snow-fencing that enclosed the jump course, and Sam had a disloyal urge to join it.

When the people in the grandstand started to cheer, he turned his attention back to the main ring and became too excited then to think about jumpers. Three horses had been selected for another workout while the rest waited in the center. One of them was Commander.

Sam felt proud of John. He was easily the best rider in the ring and he looked smart in his dark blue saddle suit and felt hat. And Commander had been clipped, brushed and polished until his liver chestnut coat glistened. Even his hock action looked good today as he made several fast, snappy passes in front of the judge, who scribbled in his notebook.

Soon the three horses were called back to the lineup, and the whole class was then sent down to the end of the ring to await the judge's decision.

"The winner of this beautiful class," the announcer began, pausing dramatically, "is Stonewall Super Chief!" The names of the rider and owner were lost in the burst of applause, which Sam joined politely. He helped swing the wide gate open, and the first-place winner came trotting out.

"Second place," the announcer said, "goes to Commander's Fanciful Delight, ridden by—" Again the rest was lost, but Sam wouldn't have heard it anyway, in his excitement. He ran to catch up with Commander, who came trotting past him with the huge red ribbon flying from his bridle.

When John had jumped down and they were leading Commander back to the barns, Sam said, "Boy! I thought a Saddle Horse class would be kind of polite and dudish—but you wouldn't get *me* into a ring with those guys! A bunch of wild Indians!"

John laughed, wiping sweat from his face as they walked. "Those were mostly amateurs—they're timid! Wait'll you see a ring full of trainers riding, in a stake class. It's suicide to get in front of those boys. They'll make a set of tracks up your back if you get in their way."

It occurred to Sam that he didn't know if there was any cash involved in winning. "Did you win any money?" he asked as they were getting Commander ready to go into his stall.

"The money's in the stake class, a thousand dollars," John said. Sam whistled. John went on, "All I won in this one was a few bucks, and to keep that I'll have to go back and ride him in the stake—if you win a ribbon in your first class, you have to. Anyway, we've won enough already to pay the entry fee."

"Gettin' away money," Sam mumbled, remembering how many times he'd heard Gramp say that.

"What?"

"That's just enough money to get you to the next track," Sam explained, and John laughed again.

"Well, that's *one* point of similarity! Horse shows aren't all that much different," he said, watching Sam's face. "Tell you what. Let's get this old prize-winning clod here put to bed, and run back and watch the jump course for a while."

When they got to the jump course's in-gate, a class was in progress. Only a few horses had completed their rounds, and a crowd of jumpers, horsemen and spectators milled around the gate. As Sam made his way through the crowd he caught a glimpse of a big gray horse. As was always the case, he felt a twinge in his chest at the sight. When he got a better look he saw that it was a beautiful animal, not the gawky, leggy colt he was hoping it might be. It happened every time. There were thousands of gray Thoroughbreds. He hurried to catch up with John, who had elbowed his way to the snow-fencing and was listening to a loud-voiced little man in a checkered hat.

"No, sir! I told Max, this morning, I said *I* ain't gonna have nothing to *do* with that crazy horse no more!"

John interrupted him as Sam came up. "Sam, this is Hank Stanley. He works for Max Goren. Hank says we're in time for some excitement."

" 'Lo, Sam," Hank said and turned back to John. "*You* know what horse I mean, John. It's the same one that killed Jack Barrows."

John frowned. "I guess I did hear something about it. Leave it to Max to pick up a horse like that."

85

"Yeah, Max can really pick 'em, all right. They don't come too rough for him. Course, *he* thinks he can handle 'em. He's even harder on a horse than Barrows used to be. But this stud's really been givin' him a good fight. Laid him right out cold, a couple of times!"

John smiled. "Really?"

The little groom smiled too. "Yeah, but it didn't knock any sense into him. He'd go right back to beatin' on that horse again. Me, now—I ain't *touchin'* it. He's a cold-blooded killer, that one is."

"Number 382 on the course, please," the announcer said. "Dappled Dan, owned and ridden by Max Goren."

"Dappled Dan!" Hank snorted. "Some name! *Dangerous* Dan would've been more like it! All that horse is fit for anymore is dog food, and he's prob'ly too tough for *that!*"

The big gray horse that Sam had noticed before was entering the ring, ridden by a grim-faced, determined-looking man. The spectators standing two and three deep around the course began to buzz. Sam could hear them muttering about the horse that had killed Jack Barrows.

"Lookit him fight," Hank said as the gray shook his head and half-bucked. "That's one horse even Max ain't gonna beat down."

The big stallion took the warmup jump, shaking his neck against the strong pull on his mouth. He had such power and stride that he gave the impression that the low jump was a mere nuisance, scarcely worth glancing at, and he cleared it with at least two full feet to spare. The watchers were quiet, engrossed by what was not a demonstration of skill but a contest of wills between rider and horse.

"Attaboy!" Sam said as the young gray galloped to the first jump, a 3-6 fence, gathered himself, and cleared it handily.

When Goren cleared the second jump, a wide spread, and had to turn the horse close to the outside fence, the crowd's well-meant cheers made the horse shy violently. To regain control, Goren hauled back on the rein for all he was worth. The horse arched his powerful neck and hauled back, almost pulling Goren right over his head. Spurring and whipping, the angry man finally got the stallion lined up for the next jump, a series of three set a stride apart.

The gray's stride was too long. He was forced nearly to a halt before each fence in the series, but his strength got him over without touching. The next jump was a chicken coop, a good-sized triangular jump made of sloping plywood boards. Again the horse fought against being turned, and three times the sharp crack of Goren's heavy crop rang out. The crowd around the edge of the course was silent in disapproval.

The horse leaped forward, approached the jump awkwardly and jumped flat-backed, his head high. It was a near thing, but he lifted and twisted his hind legs just enough to avoid touching. He landed badly, nearly stumbling, and Goren jerked the horse's head up, driving him on to the next-to-last jump, a high, straight fence. The horse shook his head, flinging ruby drops of blood from his cut mouth.

Sam glanced at John as the silence of the crowd seemed to deepen, and he knew that John shared his hope that somehow this big gray horse, fighting so hard for dignity, could win. The very silence seemed to express that hope.

The horse pounded up to the high fence too fast, but he gauged it well and sailed over with such breathtaking style that the silence was broken by cheers. The horse shied again at the sound, and again his mouth was brutally punished.

Goren forced him toward the last jump, a "gate" with a high bank rising up to it. Suddenly the horse's ears perked forward and he stopped fighting. He approached the jump eagerly. It was a long approach down the center of the course, and as he neared the "gate" he lowered his head, lengthened his stride, and charged flat out. Goren was up out of his saddle, over the horse's withers, and just for an instant he was caught off balance by the horse's sudden acceleration.

The stallion could feel this as he gathered his hocks for the jump. He ducked his head, whirled around, and crashed with savage force broadside into the heavy gate. Goren was flung off over the side. The horse's feet went out from under him on the steep bank and he went down, but he was up again almost immediately, hooves churning and muscles straining. The gray horse glanced back and kicked at the fallen man, striking him in the ribs. Goren clutched at a broken rail of the jump, then slumped, unconscious.

The gray stallion seemed to go berserk. With stirrups flying and the rein looped loosely around his neck, he galloped frantically around the course, swerving past the jumps. Several times he raced up to the frail snow fence, sending spectators scattering in panic. When some of the men tried to go to the fallen rider, the horse charged at them with bared teeth and wild eyes, driving them back through the gate.

The crowd backed away from the fence in fear. Cries

of "He's crazy!" and "Killer!" rang in Sam's ears as he clung rigidly to the top of the fence.

John tried to pull him away. "Come *on*, Sam—that horse is nuts!"

Both of them stood transfixed as the gray horse came to a halt in the center of the course, lifted his head high, and bugled his rage, challenge, and triumph. The spectacle was electrifying; the entire crowd froze. Sam's muscles tensed even more as he stared at the horse's wide eyes and imperious stance. From the edge of his mind, Sam heard his grandfather's voice. "It's the look of eagles," the old man had said.

Suddenly he broke loose from John's grip and sprinted toward the in-gate. Dodging people and horses, he raced out onto the course toward the still immobile stallion. Halfway there he slowed abruptly to a walk.

Sam approached the horse as though in a daze. Slowly he put out his hand. The scarred stallion, panting heavily through flared nostrils, his head higher than ever, watched him come. Over by the demolished jump Goren began to stir and groan, and the horse's ears flicked toward him and then back to Sam. But Sam's gaze never faltered from the horse's wide, white-rimmed eyes. The stallion let him touch him.

Sam began to stroke the trembling horse gently. A moment later the majestic head was lowered into Sam's hands and the great muscles lost their tension as the horse remembered Sam's familiar touch.

Sam led him quietly out of the ring, through the gate, and past the awestruck spectators to where John waited, pale and anxious.

"It's The Cat," Sam said. "He's scared." He leaned his head against the lowered neck.

Goren was carried past them on a stretcher, moaning and cussing. As he was loaded into the ambulance, he yelled, "I want that damn horse shot—right now!"

Sam buried his face in The Cat's silvery mane.

# TWELVE

JOHN followed Sam and The Cat back to the barns. There Goren's stablemen tried half-heartedly to take the horse, but he kicked at them so viciously that they soon gave up. Sam asked them to bring him a cooler, which he draped over The Cat. He then led The Cat away from the stabling area to a quiet grove of maples, where he led him around slowly.

John, leaning up against a tree and watching, said, "Okay, so you found The Cat. Now what?"

"They called him a killer. A crazy killer!" Sam said bitterly, hurt and angry.

John hesitated. "That's what he is, Sam. He's dangerous."

"He's just scared," Sam insisted. "He's been beat up on so much he's scared. But he's all right now."

"Just with you," John corrected gently. "Nobody else is safe anywhere near him. And, Sam—he isn't your horse."

"I'll buy him," Sam said instantly.

John shook his head. "No, Sam."

"Why not?"

"Think about it. When a horse is as badly brutalized

as this one is and still spunky enough to fight back, he'll *never* be safe. Believe me, I've seen it before. Maybe he'd never turn on *you,* I don't know. But sooner or later, Sam, he'd have to be destroyed, because he'd get *some*body."

Sam knew that was true. "But still— Can't you understand how I feel? This is *The Cat!* Look what people have done to him, what they've turned him into. And now they want to kill him for it. It isn't fair. I can't let him die that way!"

John looked at Sam's anguished eyes and turned away. "You'll have to work this out for yourself, Sam," he said.

The rest of the morning, after he'd put The Cat in his stall, Sam made his plans and began to put them into motion. First he had a long talk with the show's veterinarian. Then he got a diagram of the jump course for that afternoon's Open Jumper class and studied it. He made a trip to the entry office. He looked into Goren's tack stall and picked out a saddle he liked.

Then, in plenty of time for the class, Sam took The Cat out of his stall. Goren's stable men, with their boss out of action, had vanished. Very quietly Sam saddled the horse, bridled him, led him outside, and mounted.

As The Cat trotted across to the course with the long, low trot of the born racer, Sam saw John and Hank Stanley by the gate. He pulled The Cat to a walk and came up beside them.

John reached out and took The Cat's rein. "No, Sam," he said. "What would Jim say if I let you—"

"What's the matter with you, kid?" Hank shouted. "You want to get killed? Get down off that horse!"

"Number 382 on the course, please," the loudspeaker

boomed out. "Dappled Dan, ridden by Sam Johnson."

Sam stroked The Cat's shoulder as the crowd turned to look at him. "I'm sorry, John. But I can't let them kill The Cat while they all think he's just a crazy man-killer. I have to show them what kind of a horse he *could* have been."

Sam bent down, jerked the rein out of John's hand, and quickly moved The Cat through the gate onto the course.

"He'll have to be killed anyway," John called after him. "Don't risk your own neck—wait!"

Sam had no whip or spurs or even a helmet. He saluted the judges by pausing a moment facing them, and then began to canter in a small warmup circle. It became deathly quiet once again as this new drama presented itself. The horse's breathing could be heard clearly over the thud of hooves on turf and the creaking of leather. Sam was oblivious to the tension that surrounded him. He trusted The Cat and he knew The Cat trusted him. He glanced at the tremendous wall that was the last jump, but he felt no fear.

"He's gonna get *killed!*" Hank said, sweating with agitation. "That horse was supposed to've been shot by now!"

John took a quick breath. "He'll be all right. That horse isn't afraid of him."

"That horse isn't afraid of anything going," Hank said. "But the kid had better watch out for that wall jump!"

John looked at the course diagram posted by the gate. "It's six feet," he said, his heart sinking. "Can the horse do it?"

Hank gave a short, sharp laugh. "Not for no kid,

he won't! He'll go through it maybe, or around it, but he won't go *over* it for no kid! That horse hates wall jumps even more'n he hates everything else!"

A universal *"Oooooh!"* arose as The Cat leaped gracefully over the warmup jump.

The Cat had again shied at the unexpected sound, but this time he was gently corrected. In less than two strides he was steadily approaching the first jump, a 3-6 fence.

His gait was a flowing, loose-jointed, relaxed canter. As he neared the fence he lowered his head slightly, ears pricked forward. Without hesitation he gathered himself smoothly and soared over it.

Again he made an easy, controlled approach, to the second jump. His ears pointed eagerly, he jumped effortlessly and came down in a soft, well-balanced landing. The Cat seemed to be looking forward to each obstacle, to *want* to jump, this time.

Out of sheer exuberance he picked up speed on the turn, lunging a little. The feel of Sam's hands on the rein was trusting, not restraining. The Cat was on his own. He could do as he pleased, jump the way he really wanted to—freely, unhampered and undriven.

His next jump, over a monstrous triple bar, drew a gasp of pleasure from the crowd. He had jumped from well back, with plenty of speed and power, and never come close to touching. He pivoted at Sam's gentle touch on his right rein, gathering speed again as he headed for the plywood chicken coop.

The Cat sailed high and wide, landing several yards beyond the jump in full stride and complete control. Again an admiring murmur came from the astonished crowd.

Sam had always thought jumping was something special. Now he realized that he had never really experienced it before. Not like this. This was *flying*. He forgot that he was at a big, important horse show, riding in old jeans and sneakers; even that the horse under him was condemned. The only feeling his heart had room for was elation.

The Cat was racing now, tearing up the turf in his own kind of joy, galloping strongly down the center of the course to the last and highest jump, the six-foot-high solid wall.

Sam tensed for the first time, leaning a little too far forward, gripping the rein a little too rigidly. For a moment the high wall seemed to grow as they neared it, and his faith faltered.

As he felt Sam's hesitation, The Cat's rhythm broke for an instant, too. His ears flicked back, then forward again. Then he was charging hard, faster and faster. He raced up to the looming wall, tucked his hocks, bunched his muscles—and he was over! Sam had made it! The Cat was cantering, his crest arched and his muzzle nodding as he danced, his dark eyes shining.

The crowd erupted into wild cheering as the unbearable tension was suddenly released. Some of the spectators burst into tears.

Sam saw and heard nothing as he rode The Cat out through the gate and over to John.

John looked up at him searchingly. The boy's gray eyes were sad but peaceful. The bitterness and anger were gone.

"You got over the wall," John said.

Sam nodded and rode The Cat back toward the barns. The young veterinarian was waiting for them. They led The Cat along the aisle and into a box stall. Sam tried not to look at the open case lying on the grain box.

"How'd you do?" the vet asked, pulling on rubber gloves.

"It's all right now," Sam said.

The vet measured some liquid into a hypodermic needle. "This stuff is so potent that I don't even like to handle it. But you wanted something that would work instantly, and it will, I promise you."

"Okay," Sam said in a tight little voice.

The vet paused and looked at him closely. "Are you sure you wouldn't rather wait outside?"

Sam put his hand on The Cat's neck, then took his halter firmly. "No, I belong here."

Still the vet hesitated. "Sometimes, when you really love an animal, it's the only kind thing to do. 'The final kindness,' I call it."

"I know," Sam said.

He held The Cat's head in his arms as the vet plunged the needle home.

Sam turned and leaned his head against the wall. He had lost The Cat again. But he proved to them what a great heart the horse had—that much, at least, he had done for him. And now his own heart would have to find the courage to bear his loss once more. He dried his wet face on his sleeve and walked down to the end of the barn where John was waiting.

His gaze as it met John's was steady and level. He put his hand on John's shoulder, and the two men walked away together.

# GLOSSARY

*Barrel:* That part of a horse's body that includes its spine, rib cage and belly and extends from the shoulders rearward to the hip and flank area.

*Bay:* A common coat color in horses, one of many shades of reddish brown but always accompanied by a black mane and tail and often by black lower legs.

*Billet:* On an English saddle, a thin but very strong leather strap sewn in under the flap, to which the girth is buckled. A racing saddle has only one billet on each side; other types may have either two, three or four.

*Bitting harness:* A simple harness consisting of a *surcingle* (a padded leather strap that fits around the horse's barrel), and a *crupper* (a padded leather loop around the horse's tail with a strap running to the top of the surcingle) to keep it from sliding forward. Metal rings on the surcingle allow *long-lines* to be run from the bit through them to the trainer, who can then work the horse from the ground and still exert rein pressure straight back, as when a horse is being ridden or driven. A young horse or one with a hard mouth or certain other faults

might also wear a bitting harness in its stall for short intervals, with elastic reins attached to it, to teach the horse to flex its neck and "give to the bit."

*Blistering:* A "blister," an ointment which burns and blisters the skin, is applied to an injured leg in an attempt to bring an increased supply of blood to that area, which in turn hastens healing. It is painful to the horse, but often less painful, and of a shorter duration, than the injury it is meant to cure. Since blisters vary in intensity and usually contain mercury, they should be administered only by a veterinarian.

*Bowed tendons:* Severe strain, or sometimes even a minor accident, may cause the tendons that run up and down the back of a horse's leg to "bow" or assume a curved line instead of the normal straight one. This curve may remain to some extent for the rest of the horse's life. A horse that has had a bowed tendon in the past is somewhat weakened from it but still useful. Bowed tendons nearly always occur in the forelegs, since about two-thirds of a horse's weight is supported by the forelegs.

*Canter:* A slow gallop, with the horse well in hand. A canter is always collected. An "uncollected canter" is more properly called a "lope."

*Check-rein:* A separate rein used with a harness or a bitting harness, that runs from the bit to the back-pad, through metal rings on the bridle. The purpose is to hold the head in the desired elevated position, which not only looks smart but also helps to increase leg action.

*Chestnut:* A common coat color, one of many shades of reddish brown, ranging from almost palomino to almost black (as in some liver chestnuts) but always accompanied by a mane and tail as light as or lighter than the coat color. Two horses of the same coat color might be a bay and a chestnut, depending on the color of the mane and tail.

*Clean:* The term "clean ears" or a "clean head" suggests that the part of the anatomy referred to is well shaped and finely modeled. Also, to say that a horse has "clean legs" is to say that they are free of injuries and blemishes.

*Colt:* A young male horse may be properly called a colt until it is five years old, whether it is castrated or not. After that it is called a horse, gelding, or stallion.

*Cull:* An inferior animal unwanted by the breeder and usually sold at a lower price than that asked for higher quality stock.

*Curb bit:* A metal bar in the horse's mouth, connected at each end to another, vertical, metal bar called a *shank*. The shanks in turn have rings at each end.  When the bit is in use, the bridle is attached to the top rings and the reins to the bottom ones. Also, a chain or strap is fitted snugly from top ring to top ring under the horse's jaws. The resulting action when the reins are pulled is one of considerable leverage as the chain or strap tightens. This can be very painful, but it is incorrect to assume that the curb bit is essentially severe and used only on hard-to-control animals. When it is used by a good horseman, especially in conjunction with a snaffle in a double bridle, its effect is to cause the horse to flex its neck at the poll, collect itself, and become more delicately balanced and responsive. Abuse of the curb's leverage will, of course, spoil a horse's mouth.

*Cushion:* The surface of a race track, which is kept as soft as possible.

*Cutback show saddle:* More properly called a "saddle seat saddle," this is a particular style of English saddle, which is, however, seldom seen in England. An American invention, it is distinguished by its "cut-back" or slotted pommel; its very flat cantle; straight-cut flaps, and extremely close fit to the horse. All of this was especially designed to set off the desirable qualities of the American Saddle Horse, such as its short back, "big front," and extremely elevated head set and leg action. The rider's position in such a saddle—back toward the cantle—also is intended to show off the horse to the best advantage and to encourage a high degree of collection and "animation" by making the horse as light as possible in front.

*Dam:* A horse's mother. Its grandmother is its "second dam," and so on.

*Dappled:* Dapples may be found on almost any coat color, especially in the summer, but are most common and most noticeable on grays. They are small irregular rings of a darker color than the overall coat. They are sometimes almost indistinguishable and sometimes, as on a pale gray horse with nearly black dapples, very contrasting. A horse with dapples is said to be "dappled gray," "dappled chestnut," or whatever.

*Farrier:* A horse shoer.

*Filly:* A young female horse, from newborn to five years old.

102

*"Fire a horse"; Also "pinfire":* A hot electric needle is used to jab repeatedly a horse's leg or legs wherever an injury has occurred. The hope is that while nature cures this new injury with increased circulation, the original one will also be cured. Some veterinarians approve of firing, but many do not. A horse that has been fired usually carries "firing marks" thereafter—specks of lighter colored hair where the needle was inserted. Firing is a common practice on American racetracks.

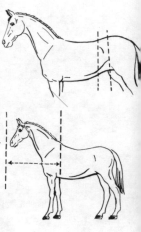

*Flank:* The tender area between a horse's hips and its rib cage.

*Foal:* A young horse of either sex, from newborn to about weanling stage.

*Forehand:* That part of a horse from the withers forward.

*Furlong:* One-eighth of a mile, 220 yards, 660 feet. According to the *Farmer's Almanac* (1972), the word was originally "furrow-long" the length of a plowed furrow, which of course was very vague. Then a furlong was established at 220 yards. But England's mile at the time was still the old Roman mile of 5,000 feet, or 1,666 yards, so for convenience's sake Queen Elizabeth I changed the mile to the present 5,280 feet, or 1,760 yards, to accommodate exactly eight furlongs.

*Gaited horse:* A five-gaited Saddle Horse. (A three-gaited Saddle Horse is generally called a "walk-trot horse.") The five gaits are the walk, trot and canter, plus two artificial gaits, the slow-gait and the rack. All are performed with exaggerated action and brilliance.

*Gelding:* A male horse that has been castrated, or "geld-

103

ed," to make it more tractable, or because it is not wanted for breeding purposes.

*Girth:* A strap, made of leather or webbing, which tightly encircles the horse's barrel and secures the saddle in place.

*To "give a leg up":* When mounting is difficult, as with a small rider and a large horse, sometimes the rider will put his left foot in a helper's cupped hands and the helper will then "give him a leg up" by lifting as the rider springs upward. This is generally preferable to a small rider hauling himself up, which turns the saddle slightly and may result in galling the horse.

*Hand:* A horse's height is measured in hands, a hand being four inches. The measurement is taken from the top of the withers to the ground. A horse that is 62 inches high is said to be 15.2 (pronounced "fifteen-two") hands, that is, fifteen hands and two inches. (Never, for some reason, would a horseman ever say "fifteen and a half hands!") A 15-hand horse is considered quite small, a 16-hand one is fairly large, and a 17-hand one is *big*. Technically, anything 14.2 hands or under is a "pony," although many owners of Arabians, Morgans, and Quarter Horses would take it badly if one were to call their horses "ponies." The show regulations vary. These breeds can be shown in horse classes even if under 14.2, but a Saddle Horse that small is classified as a pony and shown in a class such as Five-Gaited Saddlebred Pony.

*Hand gallop:* An easy gallop, faster than a canter but not so fast as a racing gallop. Sometimes it is called a hunting gallop.

*Horse:* This term is most commonly used to refer to any member of the equine species. To be more precise, however, a "horse" is an uncastrated male, or stallion. Thus the phrase "horses and mares" is proper. Thus, also, the often heard terms "horse colt" and "mare colt" are not correct, as a colt is *always* male.

*Iron:* The stirrup iron, the metal part of a stirrup.

*Leather:* The stirrup leather, a strap by which the stirrup iron is attached to the saddle.

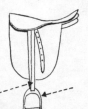

*Liver chestnut:* A coat color which is a dark shade of chestnut, more brown than red. Some liver chestnuts are, in fact, almost black. The mane and tail are usually lighter than the coat, and sometimes cream color, or "flaxen."

*Long-lines:* Extra-long reins made of leather, webbing, or heavy cord by which a trainer can work a horse from the ground, either by following after the horse or by causing it to move in a circle around him. This is called "ground-work" and is useful in starting a horse. Exercising one this way occasionally instead of riding it every day saves its back and sometimes improves leg action. Long-lines are used with a bitting harness.

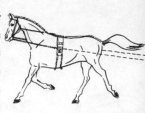

*Loose box:* A box stall in which the horse is not tied.

*Lope:* A slow gallop, sometimes called a canter. They are not quite the same, however, as a canter is understood to be at least somewhat collected, whereas a lope is "loose and easy," as, for example, the slow gallop of a western horse on a loose rein.

*Mare:* A mature female horse, over four years old.

*Morning glory:* A racehorse that is very fast in its morning workouts, but not in its afternoon races.

*Muzzle:* The soft, tender area which includes the horse's nostrils, lips, and chin.

*Neck wrap:* A band of felt or other soft, thick material that is strapped around a horse's neck at the throat, to be worn in the stall. The objectives are (a) cosmetic—by "sweating" the throat, to keep it thin and fine; and (b) after working a horse, especially in cold weather, to keep the throat from cooling off too fast and the horse from catching a chill. Highly bred, sensitive horses often wear neck wraps.

*Oakum:* Loose fiber obtained by untwisting and picking apart hemp ropes. It is used for packing horse's hooves for various reasons, sometimes in conjunction with a medication, sometimes just to provide frog pressure and keep out dirt when leather pads are used.

*Paddock:* A relatively small outdoor enclosure for livestock.

*Pedigree:* A horse's written, documented "family tree," or a copy of it. Usually only a few generations are shown, but it could be, if desired, extended back to the foundation dams and sires of the breed. There is some confusion in the popular usage of the terms "pedigreed," "registered," and "purebred." Purebred means just that—the horse is "bred pure," and all its ancestors as far back as it matters are of one breed. A registered horse is a purebred that is officially entered in the proper breed registry and has documents to prove it. The term "pedigreed" to indicate high quality is a misnomer, really, since even a crossbred horse's an-

106

cestors might be traceable, but that still wouldn't make it a purebred.

*Plater:* A racehorse that is usually entered in races for which only a "plate," a predetermined prize, is offered. Plater is not a complimentary term, because better horses are usually entered in "stakes," where all or part of the entry fees is added to the prize.

*"Run the irons up":* To slide the stirrup irons up on the leathers, and to secure them there by tucking the leathers through the irons. This is done as a safety precaution before leading a saddled horse, because "let down" or dangling irons can easily catch on something and frighten the horse. The irons are also run up for a young horse being broken to saddle, as dangling stirrups might alarm it at first.

*Saddlebred:* The popular name for the American Saddle Horse, a breed developed in America, primarily in Kentucky. (One of its earlier names was the Kentucky Saddler.) Because of its beauty and "high style," it is principally known and used as a show horse. The Saddlebred is noted for its fineness of conformation, extreme animation, exaggerated high leg action and headset, and its bold aggressive, "show horse" ways. One of the Saddle Horse's distinctions is its facility at learning to do five gaits: the walk, trot, canter, slow-gait, and rack. The last two are "artificial" and must be taught, but Saddle Horse foals are often seen to "hit a lick or two" on their own in the pasture. The slow-gait and rack are both variations of single-foot gaits, and in the rack only one hoof touches ground at a time, resulting in a very rapid, even, four-beat rhythm. It is strenuous for the horse, since extreme action is also required, but very easy on the rider, who feels only a slight vibration as the horse attains speeds sometimes over thirty miles an hour. This vibration causes the horse's high, set tail to quiver, and gaited horses were once called "shake-tails." Saddlebreds are shown in three-gaited, five-gaited, fine harness, and pleasure classes.

*Scratch:* To scratch an entry (from a race) is to remove it from competition before the race starts, usually forfeiting the entry fee.

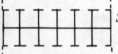

*Shed row:* A simple stable design, a row of box stalls joined together, often with an overhanging roof to keep out sun and rain. Common at racetracks.

*Snaffle bit:* A commonly used bit consisting of a metal bar, often jointed in the middle (a "jointed snaffle," then), and with a large ring at each end to which the bridle and the reins are attached. As it works only on the corners of the horse's mouth and does not exert leverage as the curb bit does, it is considered an "easy" bit. This, of course, really depends on the rider's hands. To say that a horse "goes on a snaffle" is to say that it is easy to control. It may be used alone or in conjunction with a curb, in which latter case two sets of reins are used.

*Soft mouth:* A horse that responds quickly and easily to rein pressure is said to have a soft mouth. All horses are born with a soft mouth, but sometimes abuse causes them to learn how to resist and to build up callouses.

*Sire:* A horse's father is called its sire, and to father a foal is to sire it.

*Stake horse:* In racing, a horse that is usually entered in stake races, hence a fast horse. In horse shows, in a stake class all or part of the entry fees is added to the prizes. A stake horse is one that habitually qualifies for these classes and is therefore a relatively good horse.

*Stall guard:* A structure made of metal or webbing fastened across the doorway of a box stall, allowing free ventilation and "a view" while preventing the horse's escape.

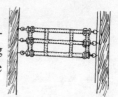

*Stallion:* An uncastrated, mature male horse, therefore capable of siring foals, although not necessarily used for that purpose.

*Starting gate:* A device consisting of a row of attached, narrow, numbered stalls that restrain race horses until the starting signal, when gates on the fronts of the stalls fly open and release the horses simultaneously.

*Stud:* (1) A stallion used for breeding purposes;
    (2) A collection of mares and one or more stallions, used for breeding;
    (3) The farm where these breeding animals are kept, along with their young offspring, as "Winfield Stud."

*Stud Book:* In the United States, the American Stud Book, which registers purebred Thoroughbreds, with their physical descriptions and their legal identifications such as tattoo numbers, pedigrees, and registry numbers.

*Tack:* Saddles, bridles, harnesses, etc., are known collectively as tack and are kept in a *tackroom.*

*Tail set:* The principal part of a tail set is the crupper; the rest is a harness to hold the crupper in place. The crupper, usually made of aluminum, is shaped rather like a shoe horn and is used to keep the horse's "cut" tail in an elevated position while the horse is in its stall. The tail set is used primarily on Saddle Horses. To show a Saddle Horse in most classes, its tail must be "cut and set." Cutting tails is sometimes thought of as a grisly process, but actually it is very simple and virtually painless. After the area is numbed, two or three tiny incisions are made on the underside of the horse's tail near its base, cutting ligaments which if not cut would prevent the tail from assuming the vertical position demanded by fashion and by show judges. After it is cut, the tail is placed in a tail set which is gradually raised until the desired height is attained. Once the set is removed for any length of time, the tail resumes a natural position, but it can be reset at any time. The cut tail does not prevent the horse from swishing at flies, as is often stated, except when it is actually in the set, and even then the horse is not inconvenienced by it, because a blanket or sheet is always worn under the tail set. A Saddlebred in a tail set and sheet is far better protected from flies than a Quarter Horse with just a short, wispy tail.

*Thoroughbred:* This term does *not* mean "purebred," as so many people seem to think. The Thoroughbred is a specific breed of horse. All Thoroughbreds can trace their ancestry back to one or more of the three English foundation sires, Herod, Matchem, and Eclipse. In the United States the breed registry is the American Stud Book. Thoroughbreds in this country are bred primarily for flat racing but are also widely used as hunters, jumpers, and pleasure horses. They are noted for their sleek, "racy" appearance, their speed and boldness. A very important contribution of the Thoroughbred is its crossing with heavier breeds to produce hunters and jumpers with more bone and substance than the purebred Thoroughbred and with less of its sensitivity and flightiness.

*Tie-chains:* Chains fastened to opposing walls or posts between which a horse may be cross-tied to secure it more firmly for grooming, saddling, shoeing, etc.

*Triple Crown:* Three major horse races in the United States constitute the Triple Crown of racing: the Belmont Stakes in New York, the Preakness in Maryland, and the Kentucky Derby. As they are all for three-year-olds, a horse must win all three in the same year.

*Trot:* A natural gait for a horse, in which two legs on "opposite corners" move forward and then strike the ground at the same instant. This action causes a distinct "up and down" motion for the rider, but the trot is very easy on the horse, which can keep it up for hours if it is in good condition.

*"Using up his race":* A horse that works out too fast or too long in the morning workout may have no "steam" left for a race in the afternoon, having "used it up."

*Walking hots:* A horse that is sweaty and overheated from hard exercise must be cooled off slowly, and the most common method is to put a light covering (a "cooler") over it to prevent too-rapid evaporation of sweat, and keep it walking until it is quite cool and dry. If allowed to stand and/or left uncovered, it is likely to become chilled or even to founder, which is a serious condition often leading to permanent lameness or the necessity for destroying the horse.

*Walkover:* A race in which one horse is so feared for its speed that there are no other entries; the lone horse merely gallops around the track ("walks over the course") to claim the prize.

*Water off:* As a hot horse is being cooled out, it is given very small amounts of water to drink at intervals, "watering it off" gradually.

*Weaned, weanling:* When a foal is separated from its dam to prevent it from nursing and is put on a full diet of grain, etc., it is said to be weaned. The average age for this is about six months. A colt or filly between the ages of about six months and a year is called a weanling.

*Weedy:* Describes a horse that is too narrow or is otherwise weak looking. Many horses that appear weedy when they are young will fill out as they mature and reach top condition.

*Yearling:* A horse of either sex that is more than one and less than two years old. A Thoroughbred's "birthday" is January first, regardless of when it was foaled. Thus a colt or filly born in January might be called a "long yearling" and one born in August a "short yearling."